The Kingdom
of Kevin Malone

Other young adult books
by Suzy McKee Charnas

The Golden Thread
The Silver Glove
The Bronze King

The Kingdom of Kevin Malone

SUZY McKEE CHARNAS

Jane Yolen Books
Harcourt Brace Jovanovich, Publishers
San Diego   New York   London

Requests for permission to make copies of
any part of the work should be mailed to:
Permissions Department,
Harcourt Brace Jovanovich, Publishers,
8th Floor
Orlando, Florida 32887.

Library of Congress Cataloging-in-Publication Data
Charnas, Suzy McKee.
The kingdom of Kevin Malone/by Suzy McKee Charnas. — 1st ed.
p.   cm.
"Jane Yolen books,"
Summary: Amy is drawn into a dangerous and disturbing fantasy
world in Central Park, created as an escape from an abusive father
by Kevin Malone, a bully from Amy's neighborhood.
ISBN 0-15-200756-3
[1. Fantasy.]   I. Title.
PZ7.C38193K1   1993
[Fic]—dc20 92-40720

Designed by Lydia D'moch

Printed in the United States of America

First edition
A B C D E

Many thanks to Stephen, as always; and to Vonda; Bethynia; Jo; and especially to Samantha, for valuable input and encouragement. And, of course, to Charles and Joan Gross, at whose apartment I set up a wonderfully trouble-free base camp during a crucial weekend.

This book is dedicated to the Corner Kids,
wherever and whoever they are.

Contents

ONE

Into the Fayre Farre

TWO OF MY UNCLES were standing by the piano with coffee cups in their hands, arguing about whether or not to sue the surgeon. I couldn't stand it.

I couldn't stand it that Cousin Shelly was dead. You don't die of a broken hip, not in your forties! People's *grandmothers* die after they break their hips. Uncle Saul, the doctor, had said that it had to be because they had forgotten to give Shelly blood-thinning drugs after the surgery, but he was backpedaling, with his big face screwed up in a very uncomfortable grimace, now that Uncle Irv was talking about suing.

I ignored the living-roomful of relatives and thought about the surgeon who had met Mom and me in the waiting room on the fourth floor of the hospital. At the time I had thought, what are *you* looking all blasted about? It's not *your* favorite relative that died while you weren't even there to say good-bye. Now I thought, maybe he had only been scared of getting sued.

I could still hardly believe it was true that my cousin and best grown-up friend Shelly Werthheim had had an operation for a broken hip and *died* of it.

And now, for seven days after the funeral, family and friends would come around to talk and cry and even laugh about Cousin Shell as they remembered her, forcing my mom to play hostess so she wouldn't just sit and brood.

It's called sitting shiva, and even nonreligious Jews like us sometimes do it when a close relative dies. It was happening in our apartment because Shelly had been an only child (like me) and her parents had died in a car crash in Florida years ago. She had no kids of her own, and she had lived with us for a year after her divorce, which was when I had gotten to know her so well. She and my mom had become very close also—"Like sisters," Mom said over and over, shaking her head and crying. Aunt Jennie was mad because she and Uncle Irv are much more religious than we are and thought they should have done the honors. I sort've wished they had.

You can have enough of anything, especially when there's tons of stuff on your mind and you're upset and everybody around you is upset and irritable too, when they aren't hugging you and burbling at you about the dead person. That afternoon I'd had enough. It was a bright Saturday in spring, and I was ready for something besides the strain and gloom at home.

I found Mom on the phone with one of Shelly's friends, crying again, and I asked if I could go out. Mom sort've gulped at me, which I took for a yes. And that was how I ended up with my best friend, Rachel, roller skating in the park where my life was changed forever.

►━◄

"Wow," Rachel said when I told her how the shiva was going. "Sounds terrible. Did your dad come home?"

"Not yet," I said. He'd gone back to Los Angeles again after the funeral to work on a screenplay and look for a house for us. I dreaded that when he did come home he would just whisk us out there with him and not even wait until the end of the school year.

Rachel threw back her hair, which was long and straight and blonde and the envy of my life. "Well, he's probably not too eager to come home anyway, not if all there is to do is sit and shiver for days and days."

Rachel's family changed their name from Beckstein to Breakstone ages ago, and she's never been a sensitive person. I just said, "Ha ha, Rock-*hell*," giving the name the Hebrew pronunciation with the accent on the "hell." She hated that.

She said, "You're so *morbid*, Amy. Let's not just sit around being *morbid*."

Which is how come we went over to Central Park, where I used to play when I lived on the West Side but where I didn't go much anymore because now we lived way over off Second Avenue, on the East Side.

Rachel led the way to this band of asphalt, running alongside Sheep Meadow, that had once been part of the park road system. Now it is closed to traffic at both ends and is used as a playing surface: volleyball at one end, roller skating at the other. I'd been promising for a long time to go skating with her. That day she lent me an old beat-up pair of her skates.

So we parked our butts on the curb and geared up.

It was a lively scene, just what I needed to clear the gloomy cobwebs out of my head. On an upside-down trash can in the middle of the pavement sat a huge boom-box, screaming out speed-of-light sales raps between blasts of music. Half of the skaters wore earphones anyway, moving to their own music.

The dress code was what you could call colorful. One guy skated in bright green sweats, somebody else in striped bike tights and a cut-off T-shirt. An older blond guy with a purple stripe in his hair, red shorts, and a red net-vest shuffled around in one small space making big moves with every part of his body but his feet. Everybody else worked around him with their eyes politely averted.

I began to feel nervous. On skates for the first time in years, I was going to be in a class by myself here, except maybe for the jerk with the purple hair. I saw my future and it stank.

On the other hand, I was hardly thinking at all about Cousin Shelly. She would have approved of my being there. She always said you should try new things.

Like death, which she was trying these days.

"I thought we came here to cheer you up," Rachel said. "Are you just going to sit there and watch me?"

So I stood and plunged into the mob after her. A slim

black kid in army fatigues did a fabulous skip and jump to avoid taking a header over my left foot. At least I wouldn't be allowed to do any serious damage around here.

I was beginning to work up a gratifying sweat when all of a sudden somebody spun by and bopped me on the arm. I stopped short, almost falling on my face when my braking-studs hit the pavement: these people didn't run into each other.

He was a dark-haired boy in a peaked leather cap and gray sweatpants with a pair of bright running shorts pulled on over them and a baggy sweatshirt, and he was skating away fast from the music and the crowd. I saw the flash of his pale face looking back at me: a familiar face, but from where?

I looked down at my arm. Something bright was stuck to my sleeve: a brooch? I pulled it off and looked at it, and I gasped. I was looking at a little bit of my past.

What I held in my hand was a pin shaped like a rose on a climbing vine made of silver-plated pot-metal and studded with tiny rhinestones. Cousin Shell had given it to me on my ninth birthday, but I had lost it a week later.

No, I hadn't lost it—the pin had been stolen from me by—oh no—the bully of my old block! Could that skater be him, after all these years?

I craned my neck, staring after him as he veered south on the paved strip, around some volleyball players. I didn't think I could catch him with the headstart he had. What was I thinking of—why would I *want* to catch him?

His name came back to me: Kevin Malone.

"Rachel!" I screamed, across the whirling crowd. "I've got to go—see you later!" And I followed Rotten Kevin off the games-pavement and along a pedestrian path through the Mall.

Up ahead, he skated hard across the main promenade and between the statues of famous old writers that sit facing each other along the Mall walkway, staring creatively into space. Then he swooped down into the dip that would carry him under one of the park bridges.

I pumped my skates (well, Rachel's spare skates) faster. Once through the arch of the bridge, Kevin would be out of sight very quickly. Without very good luck I would have no idea which way he'd gone on the other side—right, into the zoo; left, up toward the model sailboat pond; or straight ahead and out of the park onto Fifth Avenue.

He zipped under the archway and disappeared.

I mean he was there one instant, a speeding silhouette against the light at the other end of the passageway, and the next second he was gone. Vanished.

I skated down to the stone-edged entry to the arch and peered inside.

There was no sound of skates. All I could hear was some little kids shrieking at each other somewhere out of sight.

I wobbled back a few steps. The arch was made of those small, old-fashioned bricks that give "brick red" its name, with a band of grayish sandstone blocks all around the opening. On the wall facing me, a narrow metal pipe ran power inside to the lights on the ceiling.

There is a whole system of these bridges that arch over sunken pathways, so if you're on foot you can get across the roadways without being swept away by the tide of taxicabs surging through the park. Most of the bridges carry three traffic lanes, plus shoulders, on top. Underneath, where people walk through, they are deep, dark tunnels.

I poked my head inside again, squinting to screen out the bright light at the other end of the passage. The ceiling bulbs were out, but I could see two rows of fat brick pilasters, curving at their tops to make a series of round-topped niches along each side wall.

The niches were high enough and deep enough for a thin person to hide in, sort of. But there was nobody in any of them. Kevin had absolutely disappeared.

I wished Rachel had come with me.

A man came into the tunnel towing a little kid. "Shall we see if we can find echo here?" he said in a British accent. "Echo!" he called. "Echo!"

His accent struck me as so silly and prissy that my nervousness evaporated. I skated in, keeping well to the middle to avoid the slops of mud that early spring rainstorms had washed in at the sides.

"Echo!" sang the Englishman as I passed him.

Suddenly, at about the halfway point in the tunnel, a curtain of cold, blurry air closed around me and a hand grabbed mine and tugged me through the far end of the passage. I stumbled to a stop, dazzled by daylight on a grassy slope, holding hands with Kevin Malone.

"Yuchh!" I pulled free. "Kevin, you creep! What are you *doing*?"

Ignoring me, he shut his eyes and began singing, turning in place to face each of the four directions. "Welcome traveler, and fare ye well to all the farthest bounds of the Fayre Farre."*

While I stood there openmouthed, he bent down and began to search around in the grass.

---

*What I *heard* was "fair far," but I learned later that Kevin used his version of ancient-type spelling for the name of his magic kingdom, the Fayre Farre.—Amy

7

"Kevin?" I said. He didn't respond, but on the other hand he didn't protest that he was somebody else, either. "What are you looking for?"

"Your pin," he said. "You dropped it. Don't lose it, it's your passport. You have to have it to move between the worlds."

"Then you better find it," I said, "because I am sure not planning to be stuck anyplace with you."

Not brilliant, but I was so stunned that I could barely talk at all. My heart was booming around frantically in my chest, scaring me worse. Cousin Shelly had died at about my mom's age from something that wasn't supposed to kill you until your eighties or nineties. Could a fourteen-year-old person die of a heart attack brought on by sheer shock?

Luckily, there was lots to distract me from this line of terror.

We stood on top of a green hill among a whole herd of low hills. Ours was long and broad, knee-deep with tall grass, and dotted with trees. The summit where we stood was divided down the center by a wide strip of flat stone like a park pathway. But this surface was decorated with mosaics of snakes and dragons and birds, all worn-looking and drifted over with dirt. Ruins fanned out from the paving, what looked like the broken-down remains of old corridors and rooms. Grass grew everywhere. A damp, tangy wind blew.

I sure was not in Kansas anymore. Or Central Park. Or anywhere I knew!

Kevin handed me my pin without a word. I fastened the rhinestone rose through the underside of my shirt collar. It wasn't easy. My hands shook like crazy.

"Kevin," I said, "what is this? *Where are we?*"

"In the hills of the Fayre Farre," he said. "Take those skates off, they're no good on this path 'cause there's too much dirt. Hurry. The time changed while I was away looking for you. We haven't got much daylight left."

I noticed that his skates were gone, replaced by Reeboks with green dayglo laces. I didn't bother to ask how he'd changed shoes so fast. I went for first things first, like any rational person in a totally impossible situation. "What's 'the Fayre Farre'? "

He said it again, stretching the vowel sounds. Then he spelled it out: "F-a-y-r-e F-a-r-r-e, the Fayre Farre. It's my place. I made it up. Hurry!"

Made it up? Whoo. I sat down on a stone, harder than I'd meant to, and got my shivery fingers busy taking my skates off. *I am stuck in some kind of hallucination with a lunatic,* I thought, *and in my stocking feet.* But everything felt so bright, so chilly, and so spookily *real.*

I said, calmly for a terrified person, "So what's the problem with being out in the dark around here?"

"I started the Fayre Farre when I was real little, okay?" he said. "Little kids are scared of the dark, so the dark I made here has some scary things in it."

"Things," I said. "Like what?"

"Don't worry, I can handle it. Let's go." He grabbed my arm and pulled me up on my feet.

Kevin Malone had not put his grubby paws on me in years, and never with friendly intentions. I had always run when I'd seen him, but all that was years ago.

I settled for yanking my arm free. "Just hold it, okay? God, Kevin, I've got enough going on in my life as it is. What are you *doing* here? Why did you pick today to give me back my pin? How did you find me, anyway? And where's Central Park?"

"I've been tracking you for years," he said. "That old pin of yours kept tabs on you for me, and today you came close enough to reach. And something's different: your guard was down, somehow. That means something."

"What?"

"I don't know," he said. "But it means something. Everything means something in the Fayre Farre."

I was not at all delighted with the idea of Kevin spying on me *for years.* "Well, my guard is back up again, and I'm going home. Where's the park, Kevin?"

"What's your hurry?" He took off the dark leather cap he was wearing and shoved the hair out of his eyes with the back of his wrist. "Aren't you curious at all?"

"About a world you think you made up?" I said. "Even if you did create all this, which is impossible, I do know something about the imaginations of little boys"—I was thinking of Rachel's two younger brothers, the twins, who were deeply into computer-game violence—"and I do *not* want to wander around inside anything remotely related to that kind of mind. Least of all your mind, Kevin. You were a horrible little creep when I knew you, in case you've forgotten."

I turned to go back through the arch. It was right there, odd among the gray ruins: sturdy red brick with white salt deposits where decades of rain had soaked it. Rainwater dripped out of a little pipe set low on one wall near the entrance to drain the earth behind the brickwork. Wherever we were, the arch was still its plain, Central Park self, which I found very reassuring.

"You can't go back that way," Kevin said, not deigning to acknowledge my judgment of his character. "It's one time through each gateway for everybody, just one time between worlds. You just used the Willowdell. We need another arch to get you home."

Getting wobbly again with panic, I squinted through the arch. On the other side I saw not Central Park but more ruins, convincing ruins. I believed him.

"Willowdell," I said, stalling. I did not want to leave that familiar arch. "It has a name?"

"Most of them have names," Kevin said. "It was the names that grabbed me first, on a map of the park that I saw one time: Willowdell, Greyshot, Riftstone—"

The scowl that had seemed to be his main expression relaxed as he said the names. His whole face changed, taking on an open, far-off look that made me think: *Amy, you do not know this person. Maybe you did once, a little, but he's a stranger now.*

This was unnerving, but intriguing, too. What kind of stranger? Still it would be insane to stick around any longer than I had to to find out.

"What's the closest arch besides this one?" I asked, playing along.

He looked around nervously. "We'll walk over to the Denesmouth Arch. It's not far."

I started to object, but gave it up. I didn't seem to have a lot of options.

TWO

Corner Kid

THE MOSAIC SLABS of the pathway looked manageable even in socks. I tied the laces together, slung the skates around my neck and followed Kevin. Once we got started walking, I felt sort of relieved. I didn't really want to go right back to listening to my mother saying over and over that she couldn't believe it about Shelly, who was *her* cousin really and only second cousin to me; and my aunts grabbing me in these tearful hugs all the time as if that could change anything.

Soon would be soon enough. Meanwhile maybe I was ready for all hell to break loose, which could happen, in Kevin's company. He had never been dull to be around. And I realized I was very curious, even excited, about the Fayre Farre itself; I was glad I hadn't tried to go back through the Willowdell Arch, but had trusted Kevin's word that it wouldn't take me home. Home could wait.

"What *is* this place, Kevin?" I asked.

He said expansively, "I told you—my country. It's a real place, Amy. It's got history and everything, just like America or England or any place on the other side of the arches. Take these ruins, here—that's what's left of a great castle. There was a lot of battles and things fought here in the time of the First Kings."

As we hurried along, he talked. I do not remember a word. It was all fake history anyway, the kind you can find by the yard in any sword-and-sorcery novel, especially along about Volume Two or Three: kings, nobles, great warriors or adventurers messing around with magic, princes squabbling over this or that kingdom or girl or spell or enchanted weapon.

I began to expect a gaggle of wizards to shuffle by spouting spells and smoke through their beards. They always have beards and they all smoke pipes, ever since Tolkien's Gandalf set the style.

But how would Kevin even know about things like that? He was not the kind of person I associated with reading literature. Kevin had been one of about ten kids in a family down at the end of the block where I'd lived then, in the West Eighties. We'd had a cramped but sunny apartment in a fourteen-floor building halfway between Central Park West and Columbus Avenue. Kevin had lived in one of a row of what were then brownstone tenements down near Columbus.

Every time Mom or Dad sent me to a store on Columbus to get something, inevitably there would be a gang of what all the children in my building used to call "Corner Kids" hanging out on the brownstone stoops. They mugged us, for fun and profit.

Kevin, their ringleader, was skinny and fast and loud, with the dirtiest neck you ever saw. He had specialized in ambushing me in particular, and taking my stuff—money, bubble gum, my rhinestone pin.

Finally my mom had gone to have a talk with his mother, which had left me absolutely terrified that the whole Malone family would come wreak terrible vengeance on me. But I didn't see Kevin at all after that. The next thing I heard was that he had run away from home.

Then my father got his first screenwriting job in California, and though we stayed in New York—Mom didn't want to leave her job in the textile business—we did change neighborhoods. Living on the East Side, going to a new school, I forgot all about Kevin Malone.

This *was* really Kevin, wasn't it? Who else would have my old pin? On the other hand, for the old Kevin to give something back instead of taking something away was a reversal of the laws of nature on the order of dirt raining up into the sky. So maybe he had changed.

Everything else sure had. People had bought the West Side brownstones and fixed them up. Burglar bars leaking philodendron stems guarded all the windows of Kevin's building now. Last time I'd walked by there, I'd seen a huge Akita looking out of one of the bow windows. I think they're ugly dogs, but buying an Akita costs about as much as adopting a baby. The people living in Kevin's building now were definitely not Corner-Kid types.

But what type was it, exactly, who could drag me into a made-up place where I walked on real stone slabs with real grass between, among real ruins?

Take it easy, Amy, I told myself. *Just because you are having a psychotic episode brought on by the shock of Cousin Shell's completely unexpected and unfair death, that doesn't mean you are crazy forever. It will pass.* That's what Shelly used to say, shaking her head and making her earrings jingle: "Whatever it is, Amy, it will pass."

What would Shelly have thought of Kevin, I wondered. She'd been a social worker; she must have known a lot of Corner Kids.

I studied Kevin covertly as we hurried along, which was a lot more interesting than listening to what he was saying. The last time I'd seen him he'd been about three inches shorter than me, with dirty black hair chopped off at ear-level, missing front teeth, and a piercing voice.

His voice was broken now, his teeth white and even, and he had filled out with muscle. He was taller than I was, and looked especially big, because he stuck his elbows out to take up extra room when he walked with the swagger that I remembered, not fondly, from our shared youth.

He also had a shadow of a mustache, dark like his hair, and frowning eyebrows over light gray eyes. His skin was very white and clear, with what looked like a permanent flush in the form of a red strip down each cheek.

Talk about unfair; bad Kevin had become good-looking.

"Shit," he said, stopping so suddenly that I almost walked into him. Good-looking, and dirty-mouthed as ever.

At the foot of a long, gently sloping meadow bisected by our paved pathway I saw a huge wall of gray stone blocking the gap between two hillsides. A black-painted grillwork gate filled the arch.

"We're too late!" he said. "The Denesmouth is locked up for the night."

Nevertheless, he hurried down the valley. Feeling like Alice pursuing a juvenile-delinquent rabbit through a very creepy Wonderland, I trotted after him. My stockinged feet were a little sore by now, and I had to clutch the skates under my arms to avoid having them thump me to death as I ran.

I caught up with Kevin right under the high, grim wall, which was faced with sizable blocks of gray stone. He shook the bars of the locked gate. Not surprisingly, they didn't budge.

Inside, the arch was high and wide, with deep dirt verges on either side of the surfaced walkway through the middle. I could make out big barrels lined up in rows on either hand. Beyond, there was another stretch of path, gloomy green foliage, and then the stone face of another arch farther on.

"What's in there?" I asked. I realized that I'd been hoping to meet somebody besides Kevin in what was beginning to seem like an awfully empty landscape.

He stepped back, staring upward and rubbing his palms on his sweats. "The Prison City," he said.

I looked up too, expecting to see rolls of razor wire and guards with Uzis. "You made all this," I said, "and you put in a Prison City?"

"Every country has prisons," Kevin said in a hard, superior tone. "On your side it's the Central Park Zoo in there behind the double arches of the Denesmouth. Here, it's prison."

It fit, in a gloomy way: a home for caged animals was turned, in his fantasy, into a town of caged people, which was what I assumed Kevin meant by "Prison City." It was not what you'd call an ambiguous phrase.

"So we were going to do what?" I asked. "Drop in here at this prison, which was somehow supposed to get me home?"

"Something like that," he said. "But we can't get in, and there's guys around here who'd lock me up if they could and keep me for the White One. Let's go."

The image of something fat and pale like a large slug popped into my head. Somehow I did not want to pursue the subject of the White One.

"Lock you up?" I said. "In your own country?"

"I made this place for adventure," he said, sort of throwing out his chest and looking around possessively. "The whole thing, the people, the plot of the story, everything. 'Plot' means things happen, so there's enemies around, you know? Danger. Scared?"

"Nervous," I said. "Because you don't seem to know your way around your own private country."

"I know every inch of this place," he said loftily. "Every ritual, everything! So relax, Amy. There's another way back nearby, if it's where it belongs. And if not, it'll just take a little longer to find an arch you can use, that's all. Sooner or later the Battle Path will take us where we need to go."

I stood where I was, clutching the roller skates for security. "What do you mean, 'if it's where it belongs?' "

"Oh, things sort of move around," Kevin said. "Not the arches, they stay put; but other stuff kind of migrates. There's magic currents in the earth that shunt things around, like."

Oh boy, I thought. "You invented a magical land where you can never know where anything is for sure?"

He gave me a charming grin. "Magic is full of surprises. That's half the fun."

He led the way down a steep path through a tunnel of

huge old trees. Far below I thought I saw . . . was it possible? Was that why the air had such a tang to it? Where Fifth Avenue was supposed to be, marking the eastern boundary of Central Park—was that blue band on the horizon the *sea*?

I could not make my dazed mind come up with a sensible-sounding way to ask about this. The best I could do was, "So where are we going now, Kevin?" Which sounded whiney and stupid, and as soon as the words were out of my mouth I wished I hadn't said them. Luckily, he didn't seem to have heard me.

Suddenly the trees thinned out around an outcrop of black granite. From there Kevin pointed down at a shingled rooftop in a clearing below.

"See?" he said triumphantly. "I knew it was here someplace."

I saw two sharp-spined roofs parallel to each other, one on a stone-walled building and the other just a wooden porch running along the stone house's front. The main roof was straddled in the center by a spindly little steeple with a clock in it.

"The Dairy!" I said. "What's it doing down there?"

The Dairy really was a dairy once, where people bought ice cream. These days it's used for photo exhibits and to sell books and pamphlets about the park. No way could it be located somewhere east of the zoo; but then Fifth Avenue couldn't be an ocean, either.

Things moved around, all right.

"In the Fayre Farre," Kevin said, "that's an inn. We'll have some ale, or, um, juice or something, and I'll tell you why I've been trying to get you into the Fayre Farre, Amy. I think you've got a very important part to play here. Heroic, even."

"Oh," I said. "Great." We'd been doing Greek myths in

English this term. Heroes go through hell. I eyed the Dairy without enthusiasm.

I knew that your average sword-and-sorcery story had to have a scene at the inn, which was always full of spies, drunken peasants, lusty-busty serving wenches, and our traveling company of heroes. I only hoped that everybody here wouldn't talk some kind of fake Middle English.

Kevin started down a dirt path that skirted the stone outcrop. Sock-footed and still hugging Rachel's skates, I picked my way gingerly after him. *It's all a hallucination,* I thought. *I've fallen on my head on the skating pavement and I'm dreaming.*

Then I heard Kevin swear in a choked voice, and I looked up from my feet. He was running toward the gateway to the innyard, where a raggedy man was dragging himself over the ground toward us. The stranger couldn't walk because his ankles were fastened rigidly apart at the ends of a bar that looked like it was made of peeled sticks.

Socks or no socks, I ran, too.

Kevin plumped down on his knees beside the man, who could barely lift his head to look at us. I've never seen anyone so thin. He had on torn green pants and a dirty shirt that had once been bright with multicolored patches, and his hair was long, blond, and filthy.

"Kavian Prince!" he croaked, staring up with huge, red-rimmed eyes. He looked maybe a couple of years older than Kevin. "I found the prophecy." He blinked at me. "She's in it, your lady here."

Kevin glanced at me grimly.

The hurt man squeezed his eyes shut and moaned. "Past that, I can't remember. I knew the whole prophecy, every word, but then the Bone Men—"

"Later, Sebbian, tell me later," Kevin said, feverishly

struggling to unfasten the strange manacle on the man's feet. It wasn't made of wood but of two long bones twisted between the stranger's ankles and lashed tight together at the outer ends with hard leather strings.

"Wet rawhide," Kevin muttered between set teeth. "It dries rock-hard."

No way were those shrunken knots going to give. Up close, I could see that the man's bare feet were swollen so that the bone fetters had cut into his flesh, which was horribly inflamed. Now I noticed a sickly smell about him that made my throat close up.

He had somehow rubbed or chewed through the sinews holding a smaller bone manacle closed on his wrists and had gotten one hand loose. But he couldn't free his feet with his bare hands any more than Kevin could.

"Can't you cut him loose?" I asked.

Kevin slapped the sweat off his forehead with the back of his hand. "I am sworn to use no edged weapon until the Farsword comes to my hand. I'll get this off him somehow, though. Sebbian, what happened?"

Sebbian, his cheek resting on one outstretched arm, murmured, "Bone Men got me. Got away, crawled here, but innfolk had fled—nothing left, no food, no water—hiding here for days, waiting for you to come." He shut his eyes. "Beware, Prince!"

Kevin looked at me, his face white. "Amy, do you have anything sharp on you? *You* could cut these cords!"

"I don't carry a knife, Kevin," I said. It sounded awful, under the circumstances, all prissy and superior, although I certainly hadn't meant it that way.

"Dying anyway," Sebbian said. Tears leaked out under his bruised-looking eyelids. "Bone crown squeezed out all the music and the words from my poor head, except seeing your lady here, I know she's in it; she's in the prophecy. The rest is lost. Useless, should have died already—"

I felt nauseous. My wobbly gaze fell on something odd-shaped lying under the open gate, trampled in the mud—a small harp that you could hold up in your arms to play. The strings, cut or broken, curled every which way.

"Run, Lady Amy," the dying man whispered, and I saw his eyes gleaming as he twisted his neck to stare up at me. "And take Prince Kavian with you. They're coming, don't you hear them? Ah, let me not fall into their terrible white hands again!"

And then I heard a grinding, shifting sound and I felt vibrations in the earth under my feet. Pale as paper, Kevin looked back up the hill behind me and swallowed so that his Adam's apple jumped. I turned.

The flat, inlaid stones of the walkway we had come along were shifting slowly apart, and from under them drifted pale, shimmery funnels of gray powder that wavered and solidified into figures—frights from Halloween, men made of bones and rusted metal, skeletons, armored and moving.

"What?" I gulped. "Kevin, *what?*"

"It's the Bone Men," he cried, pounding the ground with his clenched fist. "The Angry Ones that Dravud Bloodhand killed with the Hurling-Stones!"

I guess I should have listened to all that fake history.

Kevin leaped up and rushed with me through the gate, across the yard, and into the inn building itself. The stink of the place went off in my head like a hand grenade—old sweat, stale food and liquor, rotten garbage.

"But what about Sebbian?" I gasped.

"He's dead," Kevin said.

Dead, I thought with a lurch, *another death*.

Kevin heaved the gaping front door shut and slammed a thick timber down into the iron brackets on either side. Then he ran to the single window and banged the shutters closed—there weren't any windowpanes—and barred them, too. The place got amazingly dark.

I could still make out enough to know that this was definitely not the Dairy I knew. We were barricaded in a long, low-ceilinged room, very dim and dingy. The stone-flagged floor was scattered with a jumble of upended furniture all roughly made of heavy, scarred wood.

I kept seeing Sebbian's pale face, and his hand with a twist of bone lashed to his thin wrist. "We're just going to leave him out there? The Bone Men—"

Kevin grabbed my arms and shook me once, hard, so that my teeth clicked together.

"The Bone Men have already done all they can to poor Sebbian," he said fiercely. "They'll do worse to you if I let them. I've got to get you out of here."

Something hit one of the shutters a whack so sharp I thought the thick wood had split. I decided instantly that I agreed.

THREE

Ash Wine

KEVIN HUSTLED ME THROUGH a low doorway into an adjoining room. Over by the back wall, which was taken up completely by a huge arched fireplace black with soot, he let me go and concentrated on undoing a knot in the corner of a lace-trimmed rag he fished out from his sweatshirt pocket. The rag looked as if it might have been a handkerchief once.

He spilled a tiny pebble into his palm and closed

his fist on it. Rays of white light squeezed out between his fingers.

"A seedstone," he said to me in a low voice. "It will make way for you. Things weren't supposed to be like this. I wanted to show you around a little, let you see what's at stake—I didn't know the Bone Men were waking here."

Somebody was, and more than waking. One wing of the shutters splintered under a shivering blow, and I got a look through the gap into the howling darkness outside. I could just make out a nightmare figure with tattered clothing whipping around the white rails of its arms and ribs.

There was a voice, too, distant and crackling faintly like a very bad phone connection. Inside the static I could hear words: "Strangers, you knocked on our rooftops. We've come to invite you in."

I thought of my heels thudding on the mosaic stones of the Battle Path and my knees turned to jelly.

Kevin shoved me inside the fireplace and reached past me with his glowing fist so that light fell on the sooty wall behind me. "There's one of the Great Ways in here. It'll take you to an arch and out."

"Then why didn't Sebbian use it?" I couldn't stop seeing the harper's face in my mind's eye.

"The Great Ways don't carry common folk," Kevin said curtly. "But they'll take you, with the rose pin to light your path."

In the other room, white stick fingers clicked on the bar he'd set across the window opening. The static voice spoke inside the wind: "If you won't come visit us, then we'll visit you. We'll drink ash wine together."

Kevin rapped the hearth wall with the knuckles of his illuminated fist, scattering velvety soot from the bricks. A section of the wall swung away.

26

"You wanted to go home—go! If the Bone Men get you, that's the end. You have to be able to move back and forth, because I can't anymore."

I gaped at him. Back and forth? *I was supposed to come back here?* In the other room, the door shuddered under a thunderous impact and another piece of planking clattered onto the floor.

"It won't be like this next time," Kevin shouted. The rushing noise and static filled the air now. He grabbed my shoulders and turned me. "Now go, go on."

"*Where?*" I said, pulling back from the inky opening in the wall. It looked like the mouth of a bottomless pit.

"Follow the passage," he said in my ear, "to the Inscope Arch. You can use any arch but Willowdell to return to the Fayre Farre, so long as you have that little brooch with you. You'll come back, Amy—the prophecy speaks of you. Sebbian said so. That's why the pin sought you out for me today. You've a part to play here; you're needed. Swear you'll come back."

A racket of hammering broke out on the roof. "God," I said, "are you *crazy?*"

He said, "I gave you your brooch back, didn't I?"

"Who asked you to steal it in the first place?" I yelled.

The whole building began to rattle like a giant snare drum played by a maniac.

"Damn it, GO!" Kevin shoved me into the passage and the stone wall crashed shut behind me.

The barrage of outside noise was cut off completely. Silence and darkness made my head spin. I have never seen blackness so black or heard silence so thick. I was buried alive and alone, except for the faint glow of the rhinestone brooch.

I fumbled it free and held it up, swinging my skates by

their laces in my other hand as a sort of weapon, I guess. The gleam of the pin lit up a squarish passage with walls of rough-cut black rock running straight away in front of me. Better that than a toast with the Bone Men in ash wine, whatever that was.

I padded down the stone passage a little way, hearing only the whisper of my own breathing and the soft brush of my matted socks on the hard floor. What was lurking just past the faint beam of the rose pin, what was listening to my trembling breathing?

It was too much, I couldn't stand it. I sat down and pulled on the skates, after brushing the dirt and crud off my sock-bottoms. Then I pushed off down that passage in a fine, heart-thundering whine of skate wheels on stone. If there was something after me down here, it was going to have to move fast.

I swooped along with the glowing pin held out in front of me in case of a bend in the passage. There were dark gaps in the walls here and there—openings to other passage-ways—which I ignored as best I could as I skated on, nerves stretched to breaking. Moss and water stains glowed and glistened on the walls. Maybe Kevin's secret passage had started out in the real Central Park as one of the sunken transverse roads that takes cars east and west across the park. The transverses are open to the sky, not closed tunnels, but they're lined with walls of this same black rock, with grass and roots sticking out of the cracks.

In the real world, the Sixty-sixth Street transverse could no more end at the Inscope Arch than it could deliver me to the moon. As nearly as I could tell, I was heading east, toward Fifth Avenue. Here, Fifth Avenue was ocean. What if this tunnel spit me into the sea?

I thought of Sebbian's ruined feet and dying eyes, and kept going—a long time. If I'd had to do any fancy footwork in a hurry I'd have been sunk, my legs were so tired.

Then the walls pulled back and the floor sloped upward and shot me out, before I could think to stop, into late afternoon light between high green banks on a paved path. There was no mistaking the smell of New York air. I was home.

I made a raggedy turn and threw my arms around a lamppost to stop myself.

I had come out under a low, pink, and gray stone bridge trimmed with a band of staggered brick-ends, like the rickrack on a child's pinafore. The mouth of the arch was small, almost prim, outlined in gray and black stone blocks. The whole thing was incredibly cozy and coy looking.

But if you go through to the other end of the Inscope Arch (as I've done since, without the rhinestone rose) you see that it's very deep and so dark that besides installing lights, the Parks Department people have whitewashed the walls to reflect as much light as possible.

And if you look back, from east to west, you see the trimstones of the opening at the far end sticking slightly into the silhouetted arch, like a curved row of huge, blunt teeth seen from the inside of a monster's mouth. I thought of Sebbian, and maybe Kevin too, chomped to shreds in that terrible mouth.

I started skating again, it didn't matter where. I just wanted to put some distance between me and all that.

It seemed as though not much time had gone by in the real world. The light was afternoonish, dulled by those rushing fat clouds you get sometimes in April; nothing like the gray evening that had been falling on the Fayre Farre when I'd left it. Time must go faster there.

Space was also stretched on the Farre side of the arches. The Inscope, which I had just come through, was only a five minute walk past the zoo from the double Denesmouth Arch (not hours of hard skating away) and less than ten minutes from the Willowdell. Fifth Avenue—Kevin's sea—was closer than that.

It was as if Kevin had created a mirror image of the real park, but packed it with extra time and spread it over extra space. All the buildings and things had been pulled loose to wander around like buffalo on a prairie; and this shifting, expanded territory was populated with minstrels like Sebbian and ash-drinking skeletons.

Now I saw everything in the real park as shadowed by Kevin's dark imaginings. Rotten Kevin had returned my pin but stolen something else precious from me: my domestic, friendly park. Give with one hand, take with the other—that was just like him, except for the "give" part.

When I got home, my aunts were cleaning up in the kitchen. The food was all put away, and there were a million dishes to be washed. The aunts were arguing in low voices about whether cremation was okay for Jews no matter how irreligious they were. They shut up when they saw me.

In the living room Uncle Saul sat slumped on the couch, frowning at his shoes. He saw me and said, "Your mom's asleep, Amy. I had to give her a sedative."

I felt weird—relieved and angry at the same time. My mom hates any kind of drugs or medicines, Uncle Saul knows that. I also felt out of phase with what he was saying because I was still thinking about Kevin and his Fayre Farre.

Uncle Saul looked at me with a concerned expression and

asked if I'd heard what he'd said. I guess he was trying not to react to the fact that I was filthy with soot and shoeless. He told me in a super-kindly voice that my Aunt Jennie would be staying over with me and Mom again, and that my dad would be back from Los Angeles very late tonight.

That was good news, anyway.

I went to my own room to get cleaned up, which was not as easy as it sounds. Soot feels soft and velvety, but it's greasy and it sticks. I was a mess. No wonder people had given me funny looks all the way home from the park.

Now what? I absolutely did not want to go back out there with my relatives. It was sickening, somehow, that Uncle Saul was sitting alive in our living room, and Cousin Shelly was dead. My strongest memories of Uncle Saul were from all the times he gave horrible, burning flu shots at Thanksgiving and tetanus shots at Passover to me and my cousins. Of course he didn't mean to be a bad guy, but how do you think it seemed to us?

But Cousin Shelly, who laughed so much and doodled endless curly plants and vines all over the paper placemats at Cannibal's, her favorite restaurant, was just ashes scattered over the Hudson River from a ferryboat.

Ash wine, I thought. Shelly was ash wine now.

My room felt cold and strange. Probably my little cousins Fran and Kimmie had been in there, snooping through my stuff. I wandered out in my bathrobe and listened at the kitchen doorway to the aunts talking about how Uncle Irv was still complaining that the funeral service had not been traditional enough for him.

Never mind that Shelly wouldn't have had a service at all. Mom had always called her, admiringly, a "free spirit," which sounded great to me. It was disgusting that Mom had given in to Uncle Irv even as far as she had. I certainly couldn't stay in the apartment, not with Mom knocked out in her bedroom and the rest of them whispering and muttering and sighing. Nobody needed me anyway.

I put on a clean shirt and jeans and used the phone in my room to call Rachel.

"Hey," she said, "what happened to you? I've heard of boy-chasing but I've never seen a girl run so fast that she left her shoes behind. You want them back, or should I give them to Goodwill?"

I told Uncle Saul I was going down to the corner store for a burger and a malt. He didn't object, or ask why I was carrying Rachel's skates with me. He also didn't mention the fact that I had ducked out of sitting shiva; but he gave me one of those looks they give you, sad and mad and disappointed all at the same time. I was very glad to get out of there.

Rachel met me as arranged, though she was late as usual. I was almost through with my malt when she arrived, bringing Claudia with her.

There was thin, blonde Rachel in a moss-green jumpsuit and her gorgeous, fairy-tale princess hair, and there was— well, Claudia, also from school. Claudia Falcone was a ditz. But not just *ditzy*. I mean there was method to her madness, sort of. Her mom had a drinking problem. Claudia talked about it with her friends as if she didn't care, but she did. Her mother went into a drying-out hospital now and then and came out again and went back in and so it went. You could always tell what stage things were at. When her mom was home, Claudia got skinny and hyper and completely scatterbrained from trying to take care of everything and make her mom happy.

When her mom was away, Claudia spent all her time in

front of the TV, eating. She got fat and slow and sort of regressed.

Now here she was walking into the drugstore wearing those Indian pants with the dropped seat and a huge droopy sweater; so her mom was in the dryer, and Claudia was out to lunch. Why had Rachel brought her?

"Here's your shoes," Rachel said, clunking them down on the table. She slung herself into the booth across from me, and Claudia shoved in beside her.

Claudia looked sort of witchy-white, and her black hair was wisping out of its barrettes as usual. Her eyes had that heavy-lidded, TVed-out look, and she was carrying—I could barely believe this—a purse made of black-and-white plush in the shape of a dog, which she put on the table so that nobody could possibly miss it.

"Thanks," I told Rachel, handing over her skates and putting my shoes down where they wouldn't be sharing the plastic surface with that purse. Suddenly Kevin and Sebbian and the Bone Men all seemed very far away.

Claudia scoped out my plate. "Are you gonna eat all those fries, Amy?" she said.

"You can take what you want," I said, "as long as you don't try to feed them to your purse."

"It's a PursePet," Claudia said, snagging herself a couple of greasy potato wedges. "From the Plush Jungle. They've got neat stuff there."

"So what's up?" Rachel said, tossing her hair impatiently.

I took a deep breath and I told them what was up.

Claudia said, "God, it sounds like *The Night of the Living Dead!*" She hugged her purse anxiously.

Rachel whistled. "Weirdness unlimited! Are you getting ready for a career in Hollywood?"

The way she said it, it dawned on me that Rachel was

jealous. *She* had the looks for TV, but *I* was moving to Los Angeles. She'd been getting weird with me ever since I'd told her about the move. Now I wished I'd never said anything, about that or about the Fayre Farre. Nobody knows how to cut you down like your own best friend.

Claudia asked, "Is Kevin cute?"

"Very," I said. "You'd love him, Claudia."

Rachel leaned over the table toward me. "So your old rose pin is the key to this magic land? Let's see it."

I put the rhinestone rose on the table between us. We looked at it. Rachel poked it with one gnawed-nail fingertip and sat back with a sigh. "It must be really tough, having your cousin die and all."

So she thought I was crazy, that I had cracked under the strain. No telling what Claudia thought; she rested her chin on her folded arms, practically lying on the tabletop, and stared at the pin.

"What are you going to do, Claudia," I said. "Eat it?"

"Of course not," she answered in a wounded tone. "Don't be cranky, Amy. It's bad for your digestion to be in a crummy mood while you're eating."

I didn't feel crummy; I felt sullen and tired and let down. "I'm not eating," I said. "I'm finished."

Claudia said sympathetically, "So you never got to hear the prophecy because the guy died. But the prophecy is *key*. I mean, there's always a prophecy in those books. You'll have to go back to the Fayre Farre to find out what it says about you."

Rachel glanced up from gnawing the cuticle of her thumbnail. "You know, there *is* always a prophecy, usually in the form of awful poetry. Did this boy say any poetry to you?"

The idea of Kevin speaking poetry even by accident made me laugh until I hiccuped. I even forgot to wonder what was going on here, that Rachel and Claudia were sort of on the same wavelength all of a sudden, and reading the same books that Rachel and I had read together.

Claudia licked ketchup off her thumb. "So when are you going to go back, Amy?"

That was too much for Rachel. "Don't encourage her," she said. "She's half out of her tree as it is, can't you tell? Amy's going to California, that's where she's going, but she's panicking about it. So she's made up this detour into some kind of dreamworld."

"Kevin is a prince," Claudia said, "and Amy's in the prophecy. She has some absolutely crucial task to do so Kevin can win back his kingdom. She's going away, like you say, Rachel, so this was his last chance to get to her. Her cousin dying made that possible, don't you see? Broke her concentration or something. Because it's all *fated.*"

Claudia was a sucker for anything about royalty. She would have sat there and listened to me babble about Kevin and his Fayre Farre all night and believed every word.

I suddenly realized that the person I *really* wanted to talk to about all this, the person who would have had something enlightening to say, was Cousin Shelly. I got a flash of her standing on the tiny terrace of her apartment, watering her potted plants with a long-nosed green plastic watering can.

And then I thought of her looking little and pale and scared in that stupid hospital bed, blinking unhappily at the cut flowers people had sent.

I guess my feelings showed. Rachel got this smirk of make-believe sympathy on her face that made me want to smack her. The idea of her really understanding what I was talking about seemed stupid. What had I expected? I was in this alone.

"Let's go," I said, getting up. "They're glaring at us for taking up their precious space."

It was getting late. We walked Claudia home first. I didn't say anything more about the Fayre Farre. They both tactfully let it drop, that and Shelly and this whole looming threat of going to the other end of the country to live in a place full of blondes like Rachel where I, with my mop of kinky brown hair and olive skin, would stick out like a sore thumb. To my relief, we mostly just complained about the humongous home-work assignments we were getting from the new history teacher.

Claudia made us wait a minute at the door while she got a book for me. She insisted, shyly, that I take it, although I was already carrying the shoes Rachel had returned. It was a short history of Central Park, with photographs and a map with all the arches shown on it.

When I got home, Mom was deep in a phone conversation with her brother Ted. Dad's plane had been delayed. I told Aunt Jennie good-night and went to bed, but I left the light on in my closet.

Maybe the Bone Men had gotten Kevin by now. Maybe if they got you, you turned into one of them. Kevin had never been my idea of a nice guy to start with. Now he might come looking for me, rattling his skeleton fingers. Which made it that much worse that he could have done—well, what he'd done: made a fantasy world turn real.

If he could do that, then why couldn't I bring Cousin Shelly back by thinking about her? I'd sort've tried since she'd died, even going once to Cannibal's and pretending she was there with me. I'd visualized her as hard as I could, pretending she was pouring some of her espresso into my milk and adding just a little sugar. Naturally, she hadn't really shown up.

Instead, I got Kevin. Give me a break. He could take his magical world and stuff it.

In my sleep Claudia's dog-pocketbook walked into the middle of my plate of fries and said firmly:

> *"When old acquaintance or old friends*
> *Twist and turn to evil ends,*
> *Even a dog-purse gives his aid*
> *Unless he's just too darn afraid."*

I woke up next morning, thinking about it: terrible poetry, if not a prophecy exactly. But the meaning was plain: better to be a dog-purse than a 'fraidy cat.

FOUR

Family Feud

MY DAD WAS HOME when I got up next morning. He sat at the kitchen table wrapped in his old bathrobe and looking saggy-faced and gray around the eyes, with a script spread out in front of him. He pushed the pages with their wide-spaced, narrow columns of type aside when I came in. Amazing that they paid him all that money for such small amounts of writing!

"Hey, Amy," he said. "Sleep okay?"

"Fine, Dad," I said. "How was L.A.?"

He wrinkled his nose. "Foul. We wouldn't be going there if the income wasn't spectacular."

I sat down across from him with a bowl of cereal. "Did you find us a place to live?"

What a relief when he answered, "Not yet, still looking. I've got my eye on a couple of possibilities, though. I brought some pictures—"

I didn't want to see any pictures. "Where's Mom?"

"Gone to Shell's apartment with your aunt Jennie," he said, sighing. "There's lots to do over there, and pretty soon people will be coming around to sit shiva today."

"Somebody could have got me up to go with them," I said. All of a sudden I felt like crying.

"Hey, Nougat," he said, reaching over to give my arm a pat. "Let them have some time alone at Shelly's place. I know you have private memories of your own about Shell, right? Well, your mom has hers to sort through, too."

Worse and worse, though he meant well. Still, it felt really good to have him home. I blew my nose into my napkin.

"How long before you have to go back?" I asked.

Another huge sigh. "I'm not sure yet. There's a story conference early next week," he said. "It's great to be wanted, but why *now*?"

I said, "Did you tell them about Shell?"

"Sure I told them. But they work under deadlines that do not move at the whim of a mere writer. And believe me, in Hollywood, there's nobody merer."

He hadn't shaved yet and looked, I thought, just a little bit like Humphrey Bogart. Cousin Shell had idolized Humphrey Bogart, and I had seen all of his ancient movies on her VCR.

40

"I think you should stay here, and tell them to go jump," I muttered around a mouthful of cereal.

"I could," he said, nodding, but I knew by his tone that he wouldn't. "But then there's a good chance my sweetheart of a daughter, the apple of my eye and the peg o' my heart, wouldn't be able to go to a decent college."

"I'll work my way through college," I said.

"As what, a heart surgeon? Tuitions everywhere are sky high and climbing, and the California state system is in trouble."

"Who says I have to go to college?" I said.

There was a pregnant pause. Dad chewed on the pencil he'd been using to mark his script. Then he said, "Your choice, of course, bunnyhunch. But you know, don't you, that Shelly particularly wanted you to go? She's left you some money, rumor has it, to help with your college expenses."

Now I did cry. Shelly had loved to travel on her vacation time, as much as she could on her not-tremendous income. Imagine her putting aside some of her funds for me, cutting days off her one-time visit to Mazatlan, or her Maine Coast cruise to study plant life in the tide pools!

"Hey, hey," Dad said soothingly. "That's what I hear, anyway. First there's some Sturm and Drang to get through, so I'm not counting your chickens and you shouldn't, either. It seems that Aunt Diane has some kind of claim on the estate—"

"Diane?" I said. "They couldn't stand each other! Shelly always said—"

"Whatever Shelly said," Dad interrupted, "Diane insists she's due something because of some ancient obligation—"

"Well, give it to her then," I yelled, jumping up from the table. "Give it all to her, let her have everything Shelly left. Who cares?"

"I do," Dad said promptly. "I've already spoken to a law-yer—"

"Oh, no!" I bawled. "Are you all going to *court* over Shel-ly's stuff? I can't believe it! It's disgusting! I can't believe I belong to a family like that!"

"Sweetheart," Dad said wearily, "*all* families are like that. Deaths and funerals, they bring out the worst in people, even people who are normally pretty okay. Nobody's at their best when they're upset. Look at your mother; look how mad you're getting right now, without even knowing the whole story." He smiled at me, but sadly. "Death hurts people a lot, it shakes them up and scares the bejaggers out of them—"

"Yeah?" I gulped. "You'd never know it from the stuff you see on TV, with people getting blown away every five min-utes. Nobody even says oops." Low blow: Dad was working on an episode of *Shakers and Breakers*, which Mom didn't like me to watch because of the violence on it. I felt my face get hot with shame over how I was acting, but I couldn't stop.

Dad, stubbly and scruffy in his old wool bathrobe, never flinched. He went right on in that reasonable tone that drove me crazy—I mean, why didn't he break down and bawl? "When people stop feeling so awful about the person they're missing, they calm down. If they're lucky and everybody tries hard, things get back to normal again."

"Fine," I said. "Well, let me know when that happens, okay? If ever."

"Amy, Amy," he groaned, "let up, will you? Look, you loved Shelly, I loved Shelly; but she's not the first person who ever died in this family, and we still *are* a family."

"Well, maybe it's a good thing we're moving away," I said. "If all anybody can think about is fighting over Shelly's things, maybe it's *time* the family broke up!"

Dad said, "Did you walk in here this morning determined to make me wish I'd stayed in California?"

No adequately blistering answer occurred to me. I stomped off into my room, got dressed, and left the apartment without saying a word more. As I walked past the living-room doorway, I heard Dad on the phone—with L.A. I could tell by the way he talked, faster than normally and laughing more.

I wanted to go someplace where if people fought, it was against a terrible evil like the Bone Men. Nobody there was running off to talk to lawyers about their dead relative's wills, either. I didn't think Kevin would have bothered stocking the Fayre Farre with lawyers.

And I hadn't felt Cousin Shelly's absence so much there, maybe because in Kevin's dream world she had never existed.

I slapped together a couple of sandwiches, pinned the rhinestone rose to the collar of my shirt, and headed for Central Park. Since Claudia's book was too big to lug around, first I went to get a park map of my own at the Dairy.

I was careful not to walk through any arches on the way there, which took some doing. The footpaths tend to lead you around a corner and into a tunnel with no warning, particularly in a rainy spring when everything is wildly overgrown so you can't even see the bridges until you're under them.

It was a relief to find the Dairy where it belonged, within comfortable sight of the brick Chess and Checkers House and a striped arch called Playmates. I came back out of the Dairy and sat down on the huge black granite slab that slopes down from the chess house to study the map. I couldn't help wondering who had given the arches their odd names: Trefoil, Glade, Greywacke?

No map from the real world could show me where I would

come out in the Fayre Farre when I went through one of the arches. But why not memorize as much as I could about their placement? And why shouldn't I choose my entrance this time, instead of just falling into Kevin's country through any old arch?

The southeast part of Kevin's fantasy land I already knew a bit: it had the castle ruins and the Prison City (where the zoo was in reality). Near where I sat, the Gapstow Bridge crossed the shallow lake below the Wollman ice-skating rink, which would mean *wading* underneath the bridge to get to the Fayre Farre, and walking—maybe running for my life— in squishy shoes. No thanks.

Playmates Arch was closest, but that was out: Kevin and I were not and never had been playmates. On the other hand, Cousin Shelly and I had gone through that arch lots of times when I was smaller, heading to or from the merry-go-round together. Even as a grown-up, she hadn't been above taking a ride on one of the tall outside horses.

The map showed three arches farther up the east side of the park. I decided on the one marked Trefoil. I must have passed it a zillion times in my wanderings in the park, but now I couldn't remember what it looked like. On the map, it was the nearest after Playmates.

Wearing my new running shoes and carrying two bologna sandwiches in a plastic bag, I folded up the map and headed east, toward the Trefoil Arch.

It was Sunday morning. Joggers ran in the park, people sat on the benches watching baby carriages, and old men and ladies threw crumbs to mobs of pigeons bobbing and gur- gling at their feet. There was no traffic on the roadways ex- cept the hordes of bike riders and skaters that use them on weekends. The East Drive took me over the top of the Willowdell Arch. Had I really skated under this archway into another world yesterday? My mind said I hadn't. My sore legs said I had.

The east end of the big lake came into view. I could see the shiny black rowboat bottoms stacked along the shore behind high chainlink fencing (people will steal anything in New York). Trefoil was right under me, with steps up to the lake on one side, paths and meadows stretching eastward on the other.

I ran down the road bank and stood on the path beneath, looking west through the arch. The near side entrance was a sort of clover-leaf shape. At the far end of the passage I could see a simple rounded opening framing the concrete steps to the lakeshore. Up on top ran an iron railing sporting lacy vines and leaves, dark against the sky.

I climbed up over the top again and looked at the other side of the arch, from the head of the steps. From this side the arch was sunk low between its green banks and overgrown on top with hummocky grass. Something unpretentious, almost hidden—that was the frame I wanted to step through into Kevin's country this time.

So I scrambled back over the top, and walked in through the cloverleaf side, clutching the rhinestone pin at my collar with one hand and my sandwiches with the other. The passageway, lying so low, was sloppy with mud. Surprisingly, the ceiling was just wood, a stained plank facing under the stone structure supporting the roadway overhead.

I looked at the ceiling because I was scared to look ahead. I asked myself, *Is this real?* And: *Am I dumb enough to do this?*

I stepped through the thick cold air curtain inside the arch—it made me shut my eyes and shiver—and came out facing not concrete stairs going up to the lake, but a high hillside covered with huge, tumbled slabs of stone, like granite dominoes tossed down from a giant's hand. Had Kevin been crazy enough to put giants in the Fayre Farre?

The slabs lay at angles just off the horizontal, like a flight of steps jolted out of true by an earthquake. Great: giants *and* earthquakes.

It was chilly again, and damp, and no identifiable time of day. I had forgotten my watch.

Now I realized that I hadn't thought about how to find Kevin in his blasted magic land when I got back into it! Suppose he was in the Prison City, or even farther away? Was I crazy, as well as a stupid idiot, to come gallumphing back here like this?

"Come on up, I've been waiting for you." Kevin stood on one of the tilted stairs about twenty yards up the hill. In his dark clothes, he was almost invisible.

I climbed, trying not to rip my jeans. A person in the normal world only has so many changes of clean clothing, let alone so many excuses to give her parents about what has happened to them all.

Kevin looked tired, though his hair gleamed beneath his cap and his black shirt and pants and dark green vest looked fresh and clean. No sweats today. I was glad I had worn a really nice turtleneck, and a clasp to hold my hair back. My hair tends to frizz in damp weather, and the air of the Fayre Farre was damp. If there's anything I hate it's having my hair bunch up like old upholstery stuffing.

"How did you know where to meet me today?" I asked. "You gave me the rose pin."

He dug out his handkerchief and untied the corner. "The seedstone drew me," he said. The little crystal in his palm looked like a stone from a jewelry setting.

Quickly I unpinned the rhinestone rose and examined it closely. Sure enough, at the very center of the cluster of petals one tiny metal cup was empty.

"You kept one of the stones from my pin? They're just paste, Kevin, they're not worth anything."

The red strips glowed brightly in his cheeks, as if somebody had smacked his face twice with a ruler. He said, "They're magic here. This one shines toward the other ones. That way I can tell where I'm likely to run into you. Hey, relax—you'll get it back."

I held out my hand. He shook his head. "Later."

"I'll remind you," I said. "Did that little stone help you get away from the Bone Men at the Dairy?"

"Sshh," he said, scowling and glancing around. "Come on, this way. Sure, the seedstone helped. Things here always help me, when they're not trying to wipe me out. I'm the protagonist so I'm mostly safe, except for, you know, ordeals and things, until the end. Don't worry, you don't have to hang around that long. How come you picked this arch to come through?"

I shrugged.

"Good thing you didn't use the Gapstow, over by Wollman Rink," he said cheerfully.

"Why, what's wrong with the Gapstow?" I asked.

"Nothing," Kevin said, "except with the arches that cross water, you never know. I put a family of trolls under one of them, and they tend to kind of wander from one water bridge to another."

"Trolls! Kevin, for crying out loud!"

"Water trolls," he elaborated for my benefit. "All ugly and slimy. Though a troll family looks out for its own, which is more than you can say for some people."

"Trolls are Norwegian," I said. "I thought you were Irish."

"You never heard of the global village?" he said in a superior tone.

"Sure I have," I shot back. "I read in my spare time, Kevin, instead of mugging people for their pocket money."

"That was a long time ago," he said, glaring down from the inch or so he had on me these days. "You're not back on your old street now, telling off a brat from the poor end of the block. The Fayre Farre is *my* place, not yours."

"I wouldn't talk so tough to someone I was asking for favors," I said.

"Maybe I won't need any favors," he said. "I won't know for sure until I've got the prophecy."

"You still don't have it?" I said. "Kevin, how long have you known about this prophecy, anyway?"

He kicked a pebble off the stair he stood on. "Only a little while. I had to find out there was a prophecy, from this dragon I fought. And then Sebbian—" He turned so I couldn't see his face. "We had a singing contest. I won him away from the White One's service, and he went off to get me the prophecy to show his, you know, his loyalty. You're not exactly coming in at the beginning of the story, you know."

"Well, let's go get the stupid prophecy ourselves, then," I said. I was not happy to be reminded about poor Sebbian, and it annoyed me to have missed the dragon. "If there's stuff I'm supposed to be able to do around here, I'd like some information about it. I don't know how it is for Prince Kavian in the Fayre Farre, but I've got school next week, and I'm supposed to be moving to California any day now. So where do we start?"

Around us were gray sky, jumbled rocks, the little arch below, and beyond it long meadows down to water and what

looked like another castle, far and lone looking. I pointed.
"Down there?"

Kevin laughed. "No, not down there. That's the castle of
a duke who'd like to nail my head to his gate and send his
own son on the quest in my place. So we'll just move along
before he finds out I'm hanging around, okay? No, not up
the Giants' Stair either. I know the way to where we have to
go, don't worry. For starters, we follow the steps across the
face of the hill."

We made our way along, Kevin showing off by walking
on the edges of the tip-tilted stones, holding his arms out to
keep his balance. The stones led to the edge of where the
forest had been sliced through from top to bottom by the
Giants' Stair, a name which seemed to answer my previous
question about giants.

"What's that?" I whispered, as we stepped off the stones
onto leaf-covered ground. "I hear something." My adrenaline
zoomed. I imagined being caught and hustled off to the castle of the ambitious duke.

"Calm down," Kevin said. "It's just our rides."

I decided to die rather than ask any more dumb questions. If Kevin was going to be coy about what he wanted
from me until we got his darn prophecy, so be it.

I was just glad to be away, moving, doing stuff, in a place
where if you died untimely, as they say in Shakespeare, it's
not because you are walking down the street and trip on a
chunk of uneven paving and break your hip, and then a blood
clot gets loose from your shattered bones and stops your heart.
It's because you're the minstrel and special friend of a hero-
prince, on your way to do him a great and faithful service,
but the Bone Men get you.

FIVE

A Seelim Ride

IN A LITTLE CLEARING near the edge of the woods
two animals browsed on twig ends. They were big,
they were saddled and bridled and shaped something like horses, but they had oval-shaped scales
all over, like lizards. One of the animals opened its
mouth and a thin forked tongue, black as licorice,
flickered out.

I stopped short. "Oh no," I moaned. "Tell me
you're kidding."

"They're tame and they're strong," Kevin said, "and we have a ways to go."

The red one sort of lifted its scales and settled them again with a faint rattle, like a parrot fluffing its feathers. The blue-green one reached forward with a hind foot and delicately scratched itself behind one ear, where its blue crest started. It rolled a flat gold eye at me.

The things were beautiful. They absolutely terrified me. I said, "I am not a rider."

"They move real smooth," Kevin said.

The creatures—seelims, Kevin called them—went into a crouch at his command. Handing the sandwiches to Kevin, I boarded the blue-green seelim. When the seelim straightened up, the ground seemed a tree-length away. I grabbed for handholds on the thin leather seat that served as a saddle.

"Where did these things come from?" I asked.

"Sebbian's family," Kevin said. "He raised them in the forest, in secret. Commoners don't have seelims."

I heard a bitter edge in his voice. "You didn't intend it to be that way, did you?" I said. "When you started the Fayre Farre? It was meant to be fair as in 'justice,' not just fair as in 'pretty.' "

He shrugged angrily. "Doesn't matter what I intended, does it? It's all changed. Here's your lunch back."

"Were they all really good friends of yours?" I asked, tying the plastic bag to a leather string attached to the saddle. "Sebbian's family, I mean?"

"I'm not here to have friends," Kevin said. "They're my people. I'm their prince, their protector."

I thought I saw a shine of tears in his angry eyes, but of course that was ridiculous. Corner Kids don't cry.

I had worries of my own. I really am no rider. In fact I have actually fallen off a horse. That is, a horse named Daisy, from the one public riding stable in Manhattan, lay down under me one day in the middle of the Central Park bridle path. It was one of the most embarrassing moments I have ever endured.

Daisy had stopped walking, thumped down on her knees with a grunt of relief, and slowly collapsed onto her side, where my leg would have been if I hadn't scrambled off. All this to screams of laughter from Rachel, who rode a lot and really knew how.

I had not gone riding since. I am a city kid. I am not supposed to ride.

But I was riding now. It was surprisingly simple. Our path went straight across open meadows and in among the widely spaced trees of the forest. It actually got to be kind of boring. Kevin was no help. He insisted on telling me the whole history of the Fayre Farre over again.

The "ancient" part was just as dumb the second time as it had been the first: Agro son of Wobbo who slew the Magenacs at the battle of Floppo, that sort of thing. More recently, it went like this: basically, there was this rich kingdom, the Fayre Farre, with a royal family and a Primordial Evil named Anglower who had been caged up by a spell after a huge battle. Generations later, the good wizard Gurd accidentally uncaged Anglower (now called the White Warrior), whose awful minions (the Bone Men) went around taking over everything.

Nobody could beat Anglower except the Promised Champion, a newborn prince of the Royal House. Gurd the Good had whisked the baby away to grow up safely on another world. However, Gurd had died before he could explain things, so the boy had grown up ignorant of his true heritage and powers.

Which left him now, well into the story proper, blundering around after a magical weapon he'd finally learned that he needed to defeat Anglower and become King of the Fayre Farre himself.

"What weapon?" I inquired. As a Corner Kid, Kevin had carried an old notch-bladed penknife with which he had threatened, from time to time, to cut off various bits of my childhood self.

"A sword," he said, "a mighty sword from the Dawn Days. It got lost in a great battle, long before Gurd's time. But the Promised Champion found the sword anyhow, even in the other world, because it was meant for him."

The Champion being himself, of course. I thought it was modest of Kevin not to pause and point this out. In turn, I refrained from asking whether any battles were ever fought in the Fayre Farre that weren't great. You know, any scruffy, scrappy, messy *little* battles.

"The sword was in a humble guise when he found it," he went on, "just as he was in humble guise himself. And being just a little kid at the time he didn't know what it was, but he knew it was precious. So he hid it away for safekeeping. But he's here, I mean I'm here. I can't get out into your world anymore. Somebody has to bring the sword to me so I can beat the White One and set things right again in the Fayre Farre." He fixed me with a significant stare: somebody, maybe me, depending on what the prophecy said.

"Why can't you go get it yourself?"

"The arches won't let me through anymore," he said impatiently. "I *told* you, I've used them all up. We just came through the last one that was open to me. But without the weapon from your world, I'll lose the final duel with the White One for sure."

I was beginning to wonder if we really needed a prophecy. Kevin seemed to know everything already. Of course for him this was the middle of the story.

"So where's this mighty weapon hidden?" I asked.

"It's someplace in my old building," he said eagerly. "I hid it there so nobody else could get their hands on it, but I'm not sure where, exactly. It seems like such a long time ago." He frowned. "I don't recall much from those days now. I only recognized you because the rhinestones in your brooch lit the way to you."

"Kevin," I said. "I hate to raise problems, but your building's been renovated."

"I know," he said. "I went there twice while I could still get through the arches. By then I couldn't see clearly there anymore. I couldn't find the sword."

"How can I find it if you couldn't?" I asked.

"Your pin," he said. "The rhinestones carry Fayre Farre magic now, after so many years here with me. They'll show you the way."

"Well, I hope they can open locks," I said. "There must be security up the wazoo in that place now. The whole West Side is like that."

"You can do it if you try," he said earnestly.

"Does this sword *look* like a sword?" I asked. "Or is it still 'in humble guise'?"

Kevin took his feet out of his stirrups and let his legs dangle. "Look, this is the great Farsword of the Fayre Farre that we're talking about. It will reveal itself to you when the time comes, that's all I can tell you. It's years ago that I hid it. The Fayre Farre is real for me now, not your side."

My side. Reality, he meant. That thought gave me shivers. What if his fantasy world stopped, for some reason, with me still in it? That is, what if a Bone Man grabbed Kevin and squashed him, bingo, just like that: where would I be then?

This was so upsetting to think about, including the Bone Man that my imagination obligingly served up in full color, that I decided to think about it later, if at all.

"So after I find this undescribable thing the exact whereabouts of which you do not know," I said, returning to the question at hand, "and that's if this prophecy says I'm the person to do it, then I have to come back here through one of the park arches to deliver this Farsword to you, right? You can't come meet me in Central Park to get it from me?"

"No," he said. "I told you."

"What about Anglower?" I asked. "Can he—?"

"Don't say his name," Kevin hissed. "Call him the White Warrior, or the White One."

"Kevin," I insisted, "can he get through the arches?"

"No," Kevin said forcefully. He glared at the sky. "No, he cannot." He sounded to me like someone trying to reinforce instructions that he wasn't sure anybody was listening to anymore.

My seelim stumbled and I grabbed leather and did not fall off, thank God. Kevin had the grace to pretend not to notice me lurching around on my saddle like a sack of potatoes.

I said, "You're stuck here with this White One, the Bone Men, and the bad duke of whatnot castle, right? In your own story, that you personally designed. You sure stacked the deck against yourself, Kevin."

"I am," he said, "and I did." He grinned a sparkly kind of grin. He knew he was good-looking. "When you're setting up an adventure for yourself, you kind of overdo the bad guys for the thrill of it, you know? Now I have to stay here and dodge them all until I get my hands on the Farsword."

Rachel and I had gone through a period of about a year when we had read all the heroic fantasy books we could get our hands on. This was after Mom had read me part of *The Lord of the Rings* out loud while I was recovering from a horrible flu bug. I had finished the trilogy myself and gotten Rachel hooked on it, too. Most other high fantasy was just bad imitation, and we'd soon tired of that. Now I wished I had paid more attention to the generally accepted form of these things.

"How long until you have to get this sword?" I asked.

"Not long," he said. "There's been omens and things. The big fight is coming soon." I did not like the way he sounded aggressive and unsure at the same time.

"How does the story of yours end?" Could Kevin have imagined a heroic fantasy with an unhappy ending?

"It ends at the Sky Castle on the Black Cliffs," he said solemnly. "The Promised Champion gets there somehow, even if he's hurt and starving and his faithful helpers are all dead or captured. He takes the Farsword and fights his way past the Bone Men to the White Warrior, and fights him as well, to the death."

I decided not to pick up on this business of what happens to the faithful helpers, which probably didn't apply to me anyway. I didn't feel very faithful.

"And he wins, right?" I prompted. "The Champion. Even though he's hurt and starving?"

"That's how I meant it to be," he said, but he didn't sound very confident.

My seelim burped and flickered its tongue, which made me jerk nervously on the reins.

"Don't pull him like that," Kevin said irritably. "He's behaving fine."

"He's a monster out of your imagination, Kevin. He's not

behaving at all," I said, but without much conviction. "Tell me something. Do you have any idea how your fantasy turned real like this?"

He shook his head, avoiding my eyes.

"You must have a theory," I coaxed.

"Well, maybe because I had no other road to go. I got in trouble in the D-home—"

"D-home?" I said. "As in, Detention Center?" Juvenile Hall? Ha. I knew it."

"Clever you," Kevin said nastily. "Bet you wouldn't know enough to survive in the lockup yourself. I did it by spending all my time in the library. Somebody had donated a whole shelfful of fantasy novels. Writing stories in my head kept me from going crazy." He tapped his temple.

"Wow, Kevin," I said. Pretty lame, but I was busy looking at Kevin in a new light. I had sometimes pictured him in the hands of lots of large cops (wishful thinking). I had never thought of him as the kind of person who would turn to books for help.

"But," Kevin went on, "some of the guys thought I had ratted on a friend of theirs. They came after me. They caught me by the back wall of the laundry room." A shrug. "I didn't have anything on me except that pin of yours, so I pulled it out. You can hurt somebody with almost anything if you're up against it, you know?

"Somehow I stuck myself with the sharp end, and boy, it hurt!" He laughed and shook his head, but his eyes had a far-off, remembering look, and not a lighthearted one. "For a minute I thought I was dying. I thought Bennie or Carlos had knifed me so fast I didn't even notice. I think I passed out. And when I woke up here I was, in the Fayre Farre instead of the D-Home. Not a bad deal, huh?"

"Looks like out of the frying pan into the fire to me," I said, thinking of the Bone Men. I turned cautiously in my saddle to look behind us, but no scraggly skeletons were in sight.

"You wouldn't say that if it had been you it happened to," Kevin said, watching me with sly amusement out of the corners of his eyes. He dug his fingers under the shoulder scales of the red seelim and scratched away under there as both animals padded uphill across an open meadow with their odd, springy gait.

A whole lot of weird ideas chased each other through my head: had Kevin really jumped somehow from danger in the D-home to the Fayre Farre, or were we both somehow inside his head while his body was still in terrible trouble back there? In that case, where was *my* body and what was happening to it while I was in the Fayre Farre with him? How long ago had he escaped from the laundry room—and *had* he escaped?

Was I dealing with a ghost here? Was he still actually back there, stuck somehow in a frozen moment of danger? Maybe he was living all of the story he'd made up in just a few seconds in the real world that translated into months, or whatever, in the Fayre Farre, and somehow he'd roped me into living it with him?

I asked, "When you were still able to get through the arches yourself, did you go back to the D-home?"

"Hey, when you get *out* of that place, you don't go back if you can help it," Kevin said scornfully. "Anyway, that's all a long time ago now. There's no point talking about it."

I decided not to argue or push for more information. In the first place, it was all so complicated and scary to think about that it made me feel as if my skull would explode. In the second place, I had a feeling that making it into—and back out of—the Fayre Farre was going to take a lot of very close attention to what was going on around me, whether I believed in Kevin's world or not.

We were now climbing pretty high. I saw distant water on both sides of the ridge we rode on and buildings here and there, far away. Some fields had dots in them that might have been cows, or whatever Kevin had invented to take the place of cows.

I said, "I'm surprised you still had this old pin of mine. It's not worth anything. Why'd you keep it?"

There was a little silence. Then Kevin said, "When I took it off you, that was a day my dad came home celebrating a bombing in Belfast. He was a great fan of the Irish Republican Army, did you know that? To hear him tell it, he was a wanted man for all kinds of mighty deeds he'd personally done against the English oppressors in Ireland. Then he kept tabs on things from here.

"That particular night he was so bombed himself by the time he came in the door, he passed out without whipping any of us kids. I kept your pin on me for good luck after that." He glanced at me sidelong. "Also, I thought those were diamonds in it. I'd never seen a real diamond, how would I know different? Anyhow, I kept it. It was small enough to fasten into my clothes where nobody could find it and take it away from me."

I didn't know what to say. Kevin's father had beat up on him? You hear about stuff like that in the news, in school even, but you don't expect to know anybody who's lived with it. No wonder he'd made up a fantasy world as a little kid— not for adventure so much as for a refuge.

Kevin pointed. "Hey, great—kaley trees!"

A line of dark trees crowned the low slope ahead of us. They had fat trunks and thick-packed leaves of a dark, glossy green.

"The nuts taste like cashews," Kevin said enthusiastically. "I tried making them out of chocolate first. I was real little then. It turned out not to be practical."

"I can imagine," I said, thinking of melted chocolate running down the branches on hot days.

"How about nuts for lunch?" Kevin said.

"Why not?" I said. "It's been nuts since yesterday."

The branches grew low enough so we could pick the nuts by reaching up from our saddles. I gave Kevin one of my sandwiches and ate the other myself. Kevin carried water in a sort of fat leather bottle slung from his saddle. He drank some and shared it with me.

We could have been on a picnic. But I was not cheerful. The empty landscape got on my nerves. My legs ached from yesterday's skating and now, in different places, from riding a seelim.

After eating we followed the road over rolling land through scattered stands of trees. Where was everybody? I was afraid to ask. We left the woodsy hills behind and started across a wide, dry plain. A hot breeze toasted my throat. I tried scratching my seelim the way Kevin had scratched his. It groaned, with pleasure I hoped. Under the scales its skin was soft and cool.

"Kevin," I said, "where are we going?"

With no warning at all, my seelim squealed and leaped in the air, and I screamed and tumbled off. I landed hard on the back of my shoulders thinking: *It's my fate, it's just Daisy all over again.*

"Let go of the reins!" Kevin yelled, jumping down before

his plunging, squalling seelim could dump him the way mine had dumped me. "Don't let him drag you!"

Both seelims sped away, leaving us standing in the middle of nowhere—but not alone.

About ten feet from us a person stood watching—a scrawny little man shorter than either of us, copper-skinned under a coating of sweat-streaked dust and ash. He wore a loincloth roughly the same color as his skin, a lumpy leather pouch slung from one shoulder, and nothing else.

"That's what spooked them," Kevin said confidently, "and he's just what we need! I told you everything works for me here." He drew himself up proudly and began to declaim, "Man of the Brangle—"

"You are pursued," the stranger observed softly, pointing past us.

We were. A shifting, swirling crowd of dust-colored animals boiled out of the ragged forest behind us. They were long-legged and long-necked with big, round faces and a funny way of lifting their heads on their curved necks, like camels, or llamas.

"What are *those*?" I said.

Kevin shouted, "Sanctuary! Sanctuary for Prince Kavian and his lady!"

The stranger didn't say a word, he simply turned and ran. Kevin swore and lunged after him, but the little guy just dropped out of sight.

"Come on, or the Famishers will get you!" Kevin yelled over his shoulder at me. Then he seemed to leap into space and vanish like the coppery man, as if they had both jumped into the Grand Canyon.

All I could see ahead was dry, bare plain. The oncoming monsters made weird squealing noises behind me—were they *laughing?* Then two of them out in front opened their mouths and I saw fangs like boars' tusks.

I shut my eyes, took a running leap, and tumbled over the edge of a bluff that was invisible until you were right on top of it. Down I slithered in a cloud of dust, into a vast tangle of thorny brush that seemed to stretch on forever.

SIX

In the Brangle

THE DRY, SPINY VINES stabbed and tore. I yelled.
Kevin dragged me in deeper after him.

"Hurry," he panted, "they can't follow us in here!"

I lumped along after him as best I could, scared
and angry. How typical of him to make our only
escape from the baddies (and I didn't have to look
again to know that these Famisher-things were not
goodies) through a forest of stickers designed to
shred you and your best blue jeans.

The little stranger was gone. Behind us, the brush seemed to squirm back into a thick, spiky tangle as soon as we had thrashed our way through it. How would we ever get out of there again, even if we could figure out where out was?

Not that I was in any great hurry to do that just then. I could hear the Famishers padding around and squealing eagerly outside the brush. As Kevin had promised, they weren't getting in—a definite plus. But if one more thorn raked me across the neck I was going to scream. I hoped the seelims had run far, far away by now. By the look of those teeth, Famishers could eat anything.

We scrambled into an open space and both collapsed, spitting out dust and twigs. My skin stung all over. For a second I thought I must have gone blind as well: then I realized that the brush grew so tall here that it closed over our heads, drowning us in brown gloom. We were completely enclosed by interlaced branches.

"I feel like I've been through a Cuisinart," I said.

"We're okay," Kevin said. "Famishers can't move around in here."

"Who can?" I said. "I'm bleeding to death. Where are we, Kevin?"

"In the Brangle," he said in a tone of satisfaction, slapping dust off his clothes with both hands and coughing. "Anglower's creatures have burned up whole forests all over the Fayre Farre. Brangle is all that grows back. The thorns hate him and keep out him and his."

"Lucky them," I growled.

"You don't understand." He had lost his cap and his hair was a dusty tangle, though not as awful as mine. He rubbed at his scratched forehead with his sleeve. "This is where we've been heading all morning. See, the Branglemen can talk with the Oldest Ones. They'll get us the prophecy Sebbian lost, the one we need, if we can find them and get them to co-operate."

"We just met one," I said. "And he took off."

"He was just a sentry posted at the Brangle's edge," Kevin said. "He's gone for the others, more important ones. I'm their only hope, they all know that. But I'm no good empty-handed; I need the prophecy that will lead us to the sword. They know that, too. If the White One's minions chase me to the Black Cliffs and I haven't got the Farsword when I meet him there, everything's lost."

"Maybe your Branglemen don't care about your sword and your battle," I said. "I mean, they live in here, right? Then what's all that to them?"

Kevin bristled. "Hey, I know what I'm doing, okay?"

"Well, excuse me," I said. "I'm just a miserable, expendable flunky without whose help you are probably chopped liver, right?"

"Sorry," he muttered.

"So how do I get home from here once we've got this prophecy?" I said wearily. I felt some sneaking sense of embarrassment, which I didn't want to let Kevin see. Here I was, a lover of Tolkien, living in a magic world that really worked—and all I could think of was getting myself back out of it again.

Kevin examined his scratched knuckles. "There's an arch in here someplace that the Branglemen keep. You'll use that."

My eyes were now used to the dimness. I could see that a lot of tunnel-like openings shadowed the walls around us.

"Well, let's look for these Branglemen, then," I grumbled, getting up. "We can't just sit here."

Something whizzed past my head and stuck into the brush

beyond me. Someone said, "Stand still or you're food for thorns!"

It was the Brangleman again—or another one, I couldn't tell. He was still (or also) shorter than I was, but he had lots of authority. In one hand he held two sticks of polished wood the size of a carving knife: throwing clubs, perfectly appropriate to people low in the pecking order in a sword-and-sorcery world (accent for the moment on "sword").

Keeping his eyes on us, the Brangleman tucked one club into his waistband, and dipping into his pouch he brought out a small, squirmy creature that he cuddled against his cheek.

The animal looked at us with little red eyes, its pointy snout twitching. The Brangleman whispered to it, then stooped and let the creature leap from his hand into the brush, giving me a quick view of a body like a very miniature greyhound. There was the faintest rustling sound, and it was gone.

The Brangleman straightened up. "That way," he said, pointing with his throwing stick.

Kevin said, "Man of the Brangle, I am Kavian the Promised—"

"That way!" The Brangleman bared brownish teeth at us, and he was not smiling.

I grabbed Kevin's torn sleeve and steered him "that way," into a tunnel. We had to walk bent nearly double, the roof of the passage was so low. There hardly seemed to be any air. All around us the brush seethed softly with tiny sounds.

The Brangleman moved so quietly at our backs that I had to look a couple of times to make sure he was still there. He was, showing his teeth and making threatening movements with the throwing sticks now.

Once he stopped us with a warning grunt and we stood there while he sniffed at the stuffy air. I did a little sniffing myself: smoke.

"That way," said the Brangleman, and off we went again.

"Hey," I whispered to Kevin. "There's a fire burning somewhere in this stuff!"

"The White One's men are always trying to burn it off and flush the Branglemen out," Kevin whispered back.

"Oh," I answered faintly, and let the subject drop. I could not talk about the prospect of being fried alive without freaking completely.

Our tunnel took a sudden turn to the right, and the ground angled down in front of us like a steep dirt driveway into a cellar. We both stopped dead. As we teetered at the top of the incline, the Brangleman gave us each a shove in the back. We staggered down, clunking into each other and making the exclamations appropriate to the situation. Kevin's language was even more raw than usual.

We fell into a shallow underground room hacked into the dirt. A sort of gate made of woven vines—with the thorns still on, of course—slid down behind us. The sharp stakes of the gate's bottom edge thumped home into deep holes in the floor.

"Man of the Brangle!" Kevin shouted. "Go tell your chiefs how you have treated the Promised Champion and his companion! They will punish you, this I swear!"

There was no answer. The Brangleman had gone.

"Where did you learn to talk like that?" I said.

He peered out through the thorn gate. "I bet I've read more books than you. I know how nobles talk."

I moved cautiously around our prison. Floor, walls, and ceiling were made of packed, polished earth as hard as stone. Little sharp edges stuck out all over where roots and rootlets had been clipped off. They bit into me when I sat down and leaned back. There was a dusty smell that made me think of live burials.

"Maybe we can dig our way out," I said, running my hands over the wall beside the thorn gate.

"With what?" Kevin said. "They cut these rooms and tunnels in the clay, stuff the spaces with brush, and set it afire. The walls bake into brick. You can't dig through it with your fingernails."

I said, "So are you just going to sit here?"

He took off his dirty green vest, folded it, and stuck it between his back and the wall. "I am," he said. "And you might do the same. One thing I've learned this side of the arches: when you get a chance to rest, take it."

"Will that Brangle-guy come back?" I asked.

"Sure," he said. "I'm the Promised Champion, the hero of the story. They need me."

"Seems to me you need them, for the prophecy," I said. "Not to mention helping get us out of here."

He chewed his lip. "It works both ways."

So they couldn't just drop him down a hole and forget about him. But where did it say anything in Kevin's world about what they could or could not do with me? I'd have bet that no instructions existed on that point.

Smoke wafted in. I coughed.

Kevin said hoarsely, "The air's better down lower."

I crouched down. The ground felt warm. "What if the fire—" My jaw locked with terror.

Kevin shook his head. "He wouldn't leave us in the path of the fire," he said, sounding so sure that I was certain he was just as petrified as I was. "The Branglemen know fire, and the green and the dry parts of the Brangle—where it won't burn and where it will—and they know how the air currents move in here."

"And they don't eat roast Champion," I said.

70

"Don't be a smart-mouth," he warned. I could see his eyes gleam angrily. "I may be just a street kid to you, but I am someone in the Fayre Farre."

"Which is nothing but a figment of your imagination, Kevin," I snapped back. I was not in a friendly mood.

"It's my country," he said. "And it's real; real enough to stick you with its thorns."

"You too," I said. "You're stuck here in more ways than one."

"Ha ha," he said. "Same old Amy, too smart for her own good. Are you in college yet?"

Well, I was annoyed and silly enough to answer, maybe because of the fight I'd had with Dad about that very subject that morning—was it only a few hours ago? Kevin and I were down there a long time, and after a while I knew pretty much what I had at the beginning.

What Kevin knew was lots more: that my mom was running a design studio for a big textile company now instead of free-lancing, and that my dad was writing for Hollywood, and all about Cousin Shelly.

Dad's new career really got Kevin interested. He asked a ton of questions about screenplays—how long did it take Dad to write one, did he have an agent, how did a script get produced, a whole lot of stuff I mostly didn't know the answers to.

Feeling cornered and ignorant about matters that I was sensitive about to begin with, I finally went on the attack. "What happened after you left home? I know you got into trouble."

"Some," he said cautiously.

"Enough?" I asked. That sounded a lot more sarcastic than I'd meant it to sound. "I mean, enough so you can do what you've signed up for in the Fayre Farre? From what I've seen, they play rough here, Kevin. They kill each other. Can you do that if you have to? Have you ever killed anybody yourself? For real, I mean, in the real world."

Silence.

"Come on, tell me."

"You don't want to know that," he said gruffly. "People getting killed, real trouble—what could that have to do with you anyhow, with your big apartment and your rich pals?"

I stared at him. "Kevin, I didn't pick where I lived."

"Well, neither did I," he said. He had detached a huge thorn from his sleeve and began cleaning his fingernails with it. "But I lived there anyways, didn't I? Long as I could stand it, I did. And I bet I stood it a lot longer than you or any of those jerks in your building would have. Bunch of wimps."

"At least none of us grew up to think we were princes and princesses," I said. Not nice, but he'd started it.

He snorted. "No point in it, for you. You were already the royalty of the street, weren't you? Whining brats with your pockets full of money—"

"Until you came along and stole it," I retorted. "Don't feel so sorry for yourself. You don't know anything about any of us. Remember Sylvia Sorensen from the sixth floor? Well, her mother killed herself, did you know that? Sleeping pills. And that scrawny boy with the lisp, what was his name—"

"Tony," he said. "Him and his baseball card collection. He was ready to sell his blood to get it back. I couldn't give those cards away, they were so beat up. They weren't worth a thing."

"Tony had such bad allergies he had to go to a special camp every summer."

"Oh boy, poor guy," Kevin sneered. "Camp! Poor de-

72

prived little creep. He stabbed me in the hand with a pencil. I still have the scar!"

"Then you must have scared him into it." I remembered Tony as a timid boy.

"It didn't take much to scare you brats from up the block," Kevin said. "Crybabies. You had everything, the whole bunch of you. We didn't have nothing."

"Didn't have anything," I corrected. "If you're going to call yourself a hero, you should learn to talk like one."

"Ha, that's how much you know," he crowed. "You know why the real Spanish, from Spain, speak Spanish with a lisp? Because they had a king who lisped, that's why. He was the king, so everybody had to talk like him. Once I've beaten the White One and taken my kingdom back, everybody in the Fayre Farre will have to talk my way or have their heads whacked off. How about that?"

"How about that?" I said. "It stinks. They're better off with old Glopgoner in charge instead of you. Who needs a hero with a chip on his shoulder?"

"When you need a hero," he retorted, "you don't stop to pick and choose. You take what you get."

"And the people around here are going to get you?" I laughed. "I'd be doing them a favor if I made sure you never find this stupid sword."

Kevin lunged forward and shoved his face in mine. "It's not stupid!" he shouted. "It's the only chance any of us have got!" He leaned back again, glaring at me. He was fast and strong as a snake, and he had scared me, pouncing like that.

"I didn't ask to be dragged into this, Kevin," I said, my heart still pounding in alarm. "Why should I help you anyway?"

He made an exasperated sound. "You're part of the story.

The rhinestone rose sought you out. Look, the Promised Champion was raised in a foreign place but there's people he knows there. Like this girl he grew up with."

Scandalized, I burst out, "You used to take my money! You call that growing up together?"

"Well, we knew each other, didn't we?" he said.

"I wouldn't say so," I said. "I sure never knew *Prince Kavian*, the hero of the Fayre Farre. Some hero."

"Hey, didn't you hear me? Watch it," he snarled. "Without me you'd be a dead duck in the Fayre Farre, even if I wasn't a prince."

"Well, I'm just a tourist," I said, "and where I come from, it's called America and even important people are just citizens, like the rest of us. So if you want me to bow and grovel and talk highfalutin baloney to you, *Prince Kavian*, you can just forget it."

We sat and glared at each other through the murk. This was not an improvement on conversation, no matter how irritating. For one thing, I noticed how thirsty I was. But I was through complaining. I was not going to play comic sidekick to Kevin's valiant prince.

Suddenly Kevin whispered silkily, "You'll do it, Amy."

"Do what?" I asked.

"Whatever the prophecy says. Because there's something I can do for you."

"Such as?" I said.

"Once I'm in charge around here," he said, "once I've overthrown the White One and taken back my kingdom, all the magic he's stolen comes back to me. It has to. I'll be able to do whatever I want here, like in the old days when I first made the place."

I did not like the sound of this at all. The boastful, vengeful tone, which seemed to promise a lot of unpleasant reprisals against anyone who had sided with the White One for whatever reason, was only part of it. There was something else, something personal and particularly aimed at me.

"What are you talking about, Kevin?" I asked.

"Your cousin," he said.

"My cousin." I echoed foolishly. A perfect wave of conviction swamped me suddenly: I should never have mentioned Cousin Shelly to Kevin, let alone allowed him to see how upset I was by her death.

"Your cousin," he repeated, "who died. Just because she's dead in your world doesn't mean she has to be dead in mine."

I sat there, stupefied into silence.

"Well," Kevin said, "what about it? Wouldn't you like to have me bring your cousin back to life, just the same as you knew her, to live as long as you want her to live? She could be nobility. She could be an important minister in my government, in charge of family welfare or something. She could be famous and rich and respected. Think about *that*, Amy."

I swallowed hard and said nothing. What I was thinking about was not bursting into tears at the thought of Cousin Shell brought to life again, surprised and delighted, and owing it all to me.

Fantasy. Nonsense. Kevin's real magic was that he had been able to somehow lull me into speaking to him as if he were a friend of mine.

"Help me win back my own Fayre Farre," Kevin said, "And I'll be able to give you back your cousin, alive and well."

SEVEN

Bad to Verse

I THINK I SLEPT. I know a time came when I found myself awake and remembering Kevin's offer, and being sure it had been a dream, or a desperate ploy on his part; nothing real. It couldn't have been real.

But I was afraid to ask. I was afraid to say anything.

About the time I noticed that I could see Kevin again, if only as a dim outline, the thorn gate rose with a rattle. We scrambled up and found ourselves facing the dawn and our Brangleman—or another one just like him.

He stood aside for us, and we went out into the tangle-walled passage.

After walking a long while through thorny tunnels, we stepped out into a wide open space with a brush ceiling at about head height (our heads, not the Branglefolks', thank goodness). In this low, roughly circular room carved out of the brush, a couple of dozen skinny figures squatted around a ring of stones in the center, a few small, shadowy animals wandering among them.

Two guys stood in the circle, throwing clubs stuck in their belts. One of them beckoned with a long, polished wooden lance.

We moved nearer. He jabbed the lance between my feet. Down I went, and down went Kevin next to me, both of us sprawling forward into the circle of stones. The guy behind us immediately bent down to fix the pattern where we had knocked some of the stones apart.

One of the little animals came and stretched its neck to sniff at my face, the way a cat will do to find out what you've been eating and not giving it any of. Others sidled up as well, and I saw out of the corner of my eye that they were checking out Kevin, too.

They were small, but their eyes were red with vertical cat-pupils that looked bloodthirsty to me. Were we going to be fed to these little monsters? I blocked that thought fast or I might have lost it right there. I almost did anyway when one of their young—I guess, since it was no bigger than a good-sized lab rat—jumped up onto my head.

I could feel its small feet digging into my hair for purchase. I swallowed a squawk of protest and stayed as still as

I could, which was apparently the right response since no-body killed me.

The guy with the lance said, "Sit."

I drew in my sprawled legs slowly and carefully. The creature clung tight. I felt less scared, but more ridiculous.

"What are you doing here, Giant?" the Brangleman said to me. He and his partner had crouched down facing us.

"Hiding from Famishers," I said. I felt a little flustered by his term of address. Giant? Heck, these people weren't so small, and I wasn't so tall. I guess it all depends on your point of view.

"And why are they looking for you, Giant?" the other guy asked. He had a puckered red scar on the side of his neck, and his eyes were sunk deep in their sockets.

Kevin broke in. "They're looking for me—"

The one behind us smacked him with his club. Kevin yelped and hunched down, holding his head.

"Only the Giant that bears the moorim will speak," the scarred one said.

I was afraid to look at Kevin. There I sat, a thirsty Giant with a moorim in my hair and not an idea in my head.

They waited.

My brain finally unfroze and gave me words to say. "This boy knows more than I do," I said. "I'm a stranger here, ac-tually. I've sort've fallen into all this, and I'm still trying to figure it out for myself."

The one with the scar smiled slightly. "A humble Giant is a rare thing," he said.

His partner said, "There are lying Giants in plenty, even among their young."

More whispering, under which I thought I heard a baby gurgling. I glanced furtively around.

At least one of the crowd near us was not a Brangleman but a Branglewoman. She cuddled a baby Brangle to nurse at one of what I realized were two rows of dark nipples down her chest and stomach. Now that I knew what to look for, I realized that a good two-thirds of the people were female.

And now that I did look, I realized uneasily that maybe *people* was the wrong word. They had broad, low skulls and their ears—I noticed with a chill—pricked and swiveled like dog's ears. The nails on the fingers of the one nearest me rose high off the fingertips and curved a little, like yellow claws. And there was a sort of light nap on their skins like baby down, but all over and standing in tufts from the points of their ears.

"The moorim will see that there are no lies," the scarred one said.

I felt the moorim's breath puff on my scalp. I wondered how the moorim would tell if I was lying or not, and what it would do if I did. My arm quivered with an urge to reach up and yank the creature down out of my hair.

"Why do the White One's helpers hunt you?" the one with the scar asked.

I figured he meant the Famishers. "Um," I said. The moorim shifted, parting my hair with its little forepaws as if it needed a better view of my follicles. I thought furiously about how to explain things to people who seemed to be even more ignorant than I was.

"Well," I said, "the White One's enemies are waiting to be led by the Promised Champion, Prince Kavian: him"—I pointed—"We think I'm here to help him get hold of a weapon to destroy the White One."

"What weapon?" the scarred one asked.

"A magic sword," I said. It was embarrassing. I mean, a magic sword!

80

The other speaker, who had a kind of dreamy look like a cat thinking about birds, said, "We know nothing of a sword, but there is a song made for this time." He cleared his throat and tipped his head back and let out this high, soft, warbling sound that was so sweet that I had to listen to the sweetness and couldn't hear any of the words. If there were words.

The Branglefolk sighed and swayed, and all their voices echoed the music in a buzzy whisper that made my eyes want to close.

"Do you know of that song?" the scarred one said when the other one was done singing.

I shook my head, forgetting the moorim for the moment. The clutch of its paws made four tight little patches of pain on my scalp.

"It's a beautiful song, though," I said. It was stunning, coming from these primitive-seeming people, if they were people.

"I made only a song about the song," he said. "Do you have a song to give for the song itself?"

I blinked. Did I have a song? Not a song, not a clue. "Us giants don't do a lot of singing," I croaked.

The singer clucked his tongue with exasperation.

My moorim had edged forward and now it bent down, twisting its neck at an impossible angle to look into my face with its bright red eyes. For a minute I got cross-eyed as well as petrified—suppose it didn't like what it saw and decided to make some changes?

"Sing," the scarred one said softly.

I licked my dry lips and stared past the moorim's weasely face. I sang the only thing that came into my frantic mind: "Oh, do you know the muffin man, the muffin man, the muffin man? Oh do you know the muffin man, who lives in Drury Lane?"

The moorim's tongue licked out—and stroked my left eyebrow.

"Not sweet, not long, but still it is a song," the one I now thought of as Singer said, the way you say, "Hmm, interesting," about a painting that you hate but that's hanging on your best friend's wall.

Scarneck said, with approval thank goodness, "It is modest to sing a question. The White One's creatures are not modest."

"Humility and modesty can be pretended," Singer said. "But the Giant has the moorim's kiss. I swallow my doubts."

I could feel the tension in the atmosphere give a little. Thank God for the moorim's kiss!

"Can I pet it?" I said, reaching up carefully.

Singer snapped out the end of his lance. I put my hand down fast.

Scarneck cleared his throat and spat rather delicately in the dust. "Perhaps you can get this weapon, Giant, but we doubt it. So if we let you go, the moorim goes with you to watch and listen. Will you carry the moorim?"

"Sure," I said, thinking, *What am I saying? Do I have to sleep with it on?* "Er, what does it eat?"

"Salt," Scarneck said. Some of the Branglefolk chuckled and whispered to each other; dumb Giants, don't they know anything? "Oils. It forages for itself. And it thinks for itself. If you betray us, the moorim will come and tell us."

"How can I betray you?" I said. "I don't even know where I am."

"Everyone can find a way to betray," he said.

"Yeah, well whose side are *you* on?" I asked, amazed at myself.

"Our own," said Scarneck, apparently not offended.

"Do you fight against the White One?"

"When we must," he said, looking around bleakly. "Many good fighters have been killed by now in this war."

Kevin spoke up, still holding his bruised head. "You said a song in exchange. You all heard her sing 'The Muffin Man.' Where's the song we get back?"

Nobody moved for a minute. Then I saw a moorim slip out of the pouch Singer carried and scramble up the leather thong that held the pouch and rub its snout on the guy's jawline. Singer frowned. He shut his eyes and said, in a sort of up-and-down chant, something that I recognized as a verse.

"A princess in mourning, a princess in gold,
A princess with talents as yet to unfold,
Shall join with the strength of the hero foretold,
And win, if their hearts be both tender and bold.
One princess must press on through terrors and fears
And solve the great riddle of using the years.
One princess must choose for a guide and a friend
A being she fears but will love in the end.
One princess must bring from her distant home's heart
A magic more mighty than any smith's art.
These three, imprisoned in walls made of stone,
Pressed to the uttermost, bounded by bone,
Using a weapon they already own,
Can bring the prince worthily home to his throne."

A prophecy if ever I heard one, bad poetry and all. I thought it would never end and got frantic trying to remember all the words. It was already blanking out of my head. In the fantasy books I've read, prophetic verses have more weight than Royal Proclamations, but you have to get the words *exactly right*.

A "princess in mourning" sounded like me; but who were all these other "princesses," and where was anything about the Farsword? We had the prophecy, and it didn't make sense!

Singer regarded me calmly. "We are even now?" he said.

"Uh, sure," I said, doing my best to hide my dismay. "Thank you."

Kevin looked as baffled as I felt. "But—what *is* this?" he said. "What 'princesses'? It's me that's got to fix things with help from you, Amy. Who are all these other people? Why isn't there anything about the Farsword?"

"Kevin, shut up," I said out of the corner of my mouth. I didn't like the way Scarneck was looking at him, head cocked a little to one side, noting—surely—that little lines of sweat were shining on Kevin's forehead; signs of very un-princely upset.

Kevin stared from him to me and back again. "It can't be right," he said defiantly. "There's nothing about me, even."

"There is, Kevin," I said. "Prince Kavian, I mean. You didn't listen. What about the last part, about bringing 'the prince worthily' and everything. Oh my gosh, I wonder if—" I saw Rachel's long blonde hair in my mind's eye. "I have a friend who might be a 'princess in gold.' " Then came a more startling thought. "And maybe the one who doesn't know her own talents yet could be—*Claudia?*"

Kevin said, his words stumbling over each other in furious haste, "Sebbian's dead, a whole bunch of great and loyal warriors have died to help my quest—and you want to bring in a pair of your stupid *girl friends?* Are you crazy? You'll wreck everything! It all has to be done right for the Fayre Farre, *my* Fayre Farre, that's our only chance!"

"Thank you for the song," I said loudly to the two Bran-glemen who faced us. "I'm sure it's perfect, as Prince Kavian will figure out for himself when he has time to calm down and begin to think straight."

Kevin jumped up cursing, freaking out right there in front of everybody.

All of a sudden they all had throwing clubs or lances in hand and had moved back from us—for room to use their weapons, I guess. I would have moved back with them gladly and left Kevin to have his tantrum all by himself, but he grabbed my arms. There was no question of getting out of that furious grip.

"Sing them another song!" he hissed. "Make them give you the *real* prophecy!"

He gave me a shake that almost caused whiplash.

I reacted automatically: I yanked one arm free and I punched him in the chest, rocking him a little and nearly breaking my hand. But he let go of me.

"Leave me alone, Kevin!" I yelled, moving back fast. "I'm not a little girl now, that you can shove around and terrorize the way you used to!"

Looking murderous, Kevin Malone took a quick step toward me.

The Branglefolk watched, commenting quietly among themselves. I heard someone laugh softly. *Ho ho*, just an afternoon's entertainment. What could I expect from people with ears they could cock like a dog's?

I made myself stand up straight, I made myself plant my feet firmly, and I raised my voice into a sort of sensible, public mode.

"Like it or not, Kevin, it sounds to me as if you certainly do need me and at least one friend of mine, probably two, to make things work out right here. And if you want *any-body's* help, you'd better start practicing some self-control."

Scarneck must have agreed, because he stepped between us. The sharpened end of his lance touched Kevin's chest. Kevin glared like a movie villain. It would have been funny, if—well, if it had been funny.

"You Giants can settle your arguments another time," Scarneck said. "Now fire is coming, and we must run away." He turned toward me. "The princess in mourning will use the archway. Kavian Giant stays with us until you bring the weapon."

A little jab of panic shot through me. "What if I can't find it?" I said. "What if I don't come back?"

Singer laughed lightly. His yellow eyes did not look amused. "Then we will trade this hero to the fire makers for some peace, if they will take him."

I looked at Kevin, at a loss for parting words. His life was in my hands, and we both knew it. Two Branglemen took hold of his arms and began tying him up with leather cords.

My heart beating fast, I walked away behind Scarneck, who padded ahead of me so quickly that I almost lost him. He was just a shadow flickering in shadowy space. What chance did Kevin have to give these people the slip here in their own maze? Not much.

Too bad. I didn't feel much like coming back to save his bacon. Kevin Malone wasn't just a tough little kid anymore. He was a selfish, bad-tempered, probably dangerous boy. I had my sore hand to remind me.

Meanwhile, here I was running after a furry little guy with pointy ears through a whispering, crackling tangle of dwarf thorn trees with a rat on my head.

I passed a patch of green on my right, then another: a whole string of gardens had been chopped into the Brangle, like a necklace of emeralds on an invisible string. A Brangle-woman looked up from digging with the pointy end of a wooden lance. She whistled and called out something. Scarneck called back and kept going.

I saw water ahead: a wide green lake half choked with tall reeds. There was a curved footbridge over a narrow neck of water, with an ornamental cast-iron rail. Scarneck stopped short in front of me, pointed at the bridge, and disappeared back into the Brangle.

I was left alone—except for the moorim—to stare out at the placid green shore opposite with its fringe of reeds. I could cross over, but I would be just as lost on that side as I was on this. My way out was not over the bridge but under it, from one side of its walkway to the other, and so, with luck, out of the Fayre Farre.

Not pausing to see if anything was lurking—I needed momentum to get me out of the cover of the Brangle, not lots of terrified thoughts—I dashed down the bank and into the water, sliding on the slippery bottom-mud as I turned sharply to cross beneath the shadowy underside of the bridge.

Cold water slapped my jeans around my legs and weighted my sodden shoes. The width of the bridge's walkway from rail to rail was only a few yards, but the water seemed to drag me back. The dank shade under the bridge coated my skin with ice.

I threw myself full-length over the last few feet of distance, and came splashing out into late afternoon sunshine, drenched with the brown water of the Central Park rowboat lake.

That's when I remembered Kevin's trolls. Now I knew

one bridge they were *not* living under. Or else they were not at home today.

And what day was it, anyway?—how long had I been gone? A man on a nearby park bench was folding up the newspaper he had been reading. By the size of the paper— as thick as a small blanket folded square—it had to be the *New York Times* Sunday edition.

Overnight in the Fayre Farre had been just an afternoon in the real world. Thank goodness: otherwise I'd have some really mammoth lies to tell my parents, and as a consequence would probably die of moorim-bites.

Shivering, I slipped and stumbled up the bank of the lake beside the stone foot of the bridge. Instead of impenetrable thorn scrub, ahead of me rose the woodsy slope of the wild little section of the park called the Ramble.

Ramble—Brangle. Kevin wasn't going to win any prizes for originality.

EIGHT

A Very Clean Moorim

So I ENDED UP walking home in squishy shoes that Sunday afternoon, with the moorim, also wet, clinging to my head. I was starving and freezing, too, since a brisk spring breeze was blowing right through my wet clothes.

I walked into the apartment. People were yelling, which was not a usual thing in my house. Mom and Dad were in their bedroom, discussing really loudly Aunt Jennie's comments to one of the cousins, of course, not Mom or Dad directly, on the shiva, which she had said we weren't doing right.

As quietly as I could, I got a package of sliced meat, a rye roll, and a jar of pickles from the fridge, and tried to sneak past the open bedroom door.

"Amy Sachs, where have you *been?*" Mom, rushing at me, stopped short in the doorway and stared. "And why are you *wet?* Where do you keep disappearing to, anyway, and at a time like this? Are you part of this family or aren't you?"

Peering at me over Mom's shoulder, Dad looked frazzled too. I tilted my head back in a way that I hoped would hide the moorim from them both without actually dumping it off backward onto the floor and spoke up as cheerfully as I could.

"I told you this morning, Dad," I said. "I went to the museum with a girl from my class for a report we're doing together next week."

No moorim-nibbles on my scalp; what was going on up there?

"Nathan?" Mom said to Dad in a dangerous tone, keeping her eyes on me.

Dad frowned. "I don't remember anything about the museum," he said.

"You were on the phone at the time," I said.

This was almost true. He had just started that phone conversation as I'd left, which was why, I guessed, the moorim was letting me get away with this part of my completely untrue excuse.

Mom's mouth turned down. "That I can believe: talking with those crap-artists in Los Angeles."

Dad chose not to be deflected from the topic under discussion.

"So where *have* you been?" he asked.

"I told you, I went to the museum with my friend Joyce,"
I improvised. "And after, we were playing around the foun-
tains out in front and the wind blew the water all over the
place and got us wet. Anyway, it was more fun than sitting
shiva."

The looks on their faces told me to correct that last part
fast. "I mean, I needed a break, you know? What's the big
deal, anyway? It was schoolwork."

"Joyce?" Mom said. "I don't remember meeting a girl named
Joyce."

Dad said, "You don't look as if you've been at a museum.
You look as if you've been running relay races in a barbed-
wire factory."

"Underwater," Mom added.

I was fed up. "Well, I'm glad everybody's so glad to see
me," I said. "I wouldn't have come home at all if I'd known I
was in for a police interrogation."

Okay, I was being pretty uncool here; but I was really
distracted, wondering when the darn moorim was going to
chomp down on me for the lies I was telling. Maybe only
lies told to actual Branglemen counted?

Mom pointed. "Amy, go get cleaned up. I don't want you
sitting down to dinner looking like some—some street waif!"

She went back into the bedroom with Dad, starting some
comment about what a pain in the neck Aunt Jennie was.
Their door closed. I breathed in deeply—the moorim seemed
to sigh a tiny warm sigh into my hair, too—and I bolted for
my own room.

At last.

While I ate what I'd grabbed from the kitchen, sitting on
my bed, I hurriedly made notes on what I could remember

of the prophecy. I didn't like the sound of it one bit. Aside from the junk about princesses, there was that line about being "imprisoned." And what weapon did we already have? It made no sense. Prophecies are supposed to be sort of obscure, but this one seemed like pure, frustrating gobbledygook.

In the shower I thought things over.

What was important was that I was home now, out of the Fayre Farre, with a souvenir to remind me that it had not been just a dream. The moorim, nattering frantically to itself in a high, breathy voice, had one foot braced on my left ear and was trying to winch its way back up to the top of my skull via my wet, slippery hair, hanks of which were clutched painfully in its other three feet. I finally gave the creature a boost with my hand for fear of being plucked bald by its desperate mountaineering.

But, moorim or no moorim, I didn't absolutely have to go *back*, did I? The prophecy was only a prophecy, not a history of something that had already happened. Even the moorim couldn't *make* me return. Probably.

So what did I want to do about Kevin and his Fayre Farre? What should I do? Anything?

I mean, a magic sword, for Pete's sake, and Kevin the Promised Champion! Should he be in charge of a whole world? What kind of supreme ruler would he be to Scarneck and Singer, and Sebbian's poor bereaved family, and all the giants and trolls he'd stocked the place with?

Could I even be sure that Kevin really was the hero of the story? For all I knew, Anglower was a freedom fighter leading an uprising against a rotten royal family of which Prince Kavian was the current and terrible heir apparent.

God, it was so *complicated*. And it was so real.

It now seemed obvious to me that if the Branglemen decided to chop Kevin's head off because I didn't play my part in the epic of the Fayre Farre, well, Kevin's head would be off. Really. In his world *and* mine. My smarting knuckles and millions of scratches told me that, not to mention the moorim's warm little weight on my skull.

Speaking of which: I turned the shower on harder and hotter, to see what would happen. But the moorim hung on tightly, making pathetic muffled moans into my scalp. Since I didn't really want to drown it, I let up on the water. The moorim shifted its sopping little weight higher onto the top of my head and lay there gasping faintly.

I needed someone wise and understanding to consult with; but talking to Cousin Shell was not an option.

I couldn't dry my hair because the moorim kept skipping around up there and kind of grabbing my fingers when I got too close. It had sharp little claws, and small rivulets of water seeped off it into my hair and down my skin.

Pulling on my bathrobe, I flopped down on my bed with Claudia's park book. The moorim sat on my head and fidgeted. Maybe it was grooming itself, combing its fur with its tiny clawed fingers. I didn't let myself think about what it might be looking for.

Hours later I heard my mother's quick footsteps heading my way. The moorim dove for cover, deeper into the back of my hair, which had dried into a Brangle-like mass without the smoothing effects of my hair dryer, brush, or comb.

"Amy?" Mom said, sticking her head in my bedroom doorway. She looked composed but red-eyed. I braced myself for the worst.

"Have you been sitting in here alone thinking about

Shelly?" she said, taking the park book out of my hands and looking at it. "No, I guess not. Well, come on—it's dinner-time."

"I'm really not hungry," I said, trying to look meek and contrite.

She sat on the end of my bed and looked at me. "I don't understand you. I thought you were close to Shelly, but you're acting so selfish and unpredictable—running off yesterday with Rachel, and today with some kid I've never even heard of, and coming back here looking like a drowned rat!"

"I told you what happened," I mumbled.

"You're not dressed," she said. "Are you sick? Did you catch cold, getting wet like that?"

"I'm fine," I said.

"This girl—Joyce—what's her last name? I'm going to call up her mother." Her eyes narrowed. "What's that on your head?"

"It's a hamster," I said.

She stared incredulously. "A *hamster?*"

The moorim lay very still. Was it sick? In shock over the humongous lies I was telling? Maybe I had burned out its judgmental system by overloading it.

"It's a toy, actually," I gabbled brightly. "Somebody was handing them out in school last week, a kid in the Modern Issues elective who's doing a paper on deviant experience."

"Deviant experience?" my mom said. "Wearing animals on your head? That's a bit much even for the Cornford School. Teaching kids about deviance isn't on the curriculum that I remember, and frankly I'm not sure it's what your father and I meant your tuition money to pay for."

As she spoke, I was thinking: tomorrow was a school day. If I wanted a chance to tell Rachel about the prophecy without the whole world poking their nose into our business, I was going to have to do it now, tonight. If I could just get away from my mom. . . . I got up and began digging clean clothes out of my closet.

Mom watched me thoughtfully. "Amy," she said, "while in some ways it's rather diverting, and God knows I need diversion these days, I am not very happy seeing you walk around with a rodent-doll on your head. How long are you going to wear it?"

"Just today," I said. "I have to test people's reactions to it for twenty-four hours."

"I think I smell baloney," Mom said dangerously.

"Where did Dad go?" I asked. "He's not due back in Los Angeles until tomorrow, he told me."

"He went over to Shelly's apartment," Mom said, her eyes tearing up again. "I left my keys there, and I just couldn't bring myself to go back again—where are *you* going? I'm about to put dinner on the table."

"I have to go out," I said, dressing fast. "Rachel is thinking of running for class president. She wants me to help plan her campaign."

Rachel, in school politics? What a hoot! But my lie brought no response from the moorim. Maybe it had caught pneumonia in the shower and expired? I could feel it sprawled on my scalp like a miniature tigerskin rug. It made a soft humming noise, like purring. I hoped Mom couldn't hear it.

"You just spent all day running around with this Joyce from school instead of being here with us," Mom said as I sidled past her and headed for the front door. "Friends are important, but at a time like this you have to think of your family, Amy. Can't Rachel's political career wait an evening?"

Mom thought Rachel was snooty and spoiled and fixated

on her looks, which was true but not exactly in the way Mom thought. In fact, Rachel lived for the day when she could get her nose fixed because she thought it ruined her looks. We'd argued about all this before. I wasn't in any mood to take up the subject again, so Mom tore on uninterrupted.

"I think you should stay here tonight"—Her eyes focused on my head again and widened. "It moved!"

"Oh, that's the fun part," I said. "They're plastic. I squeeze a bulb in my pocket and the hamster wiggles."

The moorim not only wiggled, it nuzzled my ear. I felt triumphant: *Take that, Branglemen! You think you're so smart!*

Mom's jaw dropped. "That thing," she said flatly, "is alive. Get rid of it, Amy. I don't care what arcane science project they are doing at that school, you are not going around with a rat on your head."

"It's not a rat, it's a moorim." I backed down the hallway away from her. "And I'm stuck with it until I can do something about Kevin and the Fayre Farre. YOW!"

The moorim had given my ear a sharp nip with its needly little teeth, and suddenly—as I zipped out the door of our apartment with Mom yelling something after me—I realized what had happened. I was in a sort of backward pattern here, a mirror effect. In the Fayre Farre the moorim insisted on truth, but in the real world it allowed only lies! Welcome through the looking glass, only it's this side that's backward.

NINE

The Plush Jungle

I HEADED DOWN Second Avenue toward Rachel's, hoping she'd be home. I should have phoned first, but I hadn't been thinking too clearly. Of course with the moorim on my head, when I found her I wouldn't be able to utter one true sentence unless I was ready to get my poor head chewed to a nubbin.

The moorim tugged on my hair.

"Whaddaya want?" I howled, trying to look up into my own hairline.

The moorim squeaked distressfully and pulled harder. Had it gone crazy? Maybe I should lie down like Daisy, since the creature was riding me like a horse. That was it! The moorim was trying to *steer* me.

Might as well be steered. And so I ended up outside the Plush Jungle, on Lexington Avenue, at about six P.M. on Sunday. The place was always open at weird hours. I guess the owner was a free spirit, like Shell.

I am too old for stuffed animals, even very expensive ones that people give to each other in the throes of infantile love. My own dad bought something there for Mom after his third trip to Los Angeles, as a peace offering I guess. I won't say what it was—it's too embarrassing. There are times when one's parents are unbelievable.

There was an audience outside the store as usual. Two women studied the window display, commenting admiringly in a foreign language I didn't recognize.

What we had here was a beach scene: a large stuffed gorilla lazed in a hammock with a fake drink in its foot among stuffed palm trees that were being climbed and variously nestled into by smaller toys, like a couple of sloths and a goggle-eyed python. Two stuffed dolphins and a shark lolled among crepe-paper waves, cheered on by a crowd of stuffed penguins.

Rachel was inside talking to the owner, a round, short woman who wore a frilly pink housecoat type of dress.

I walked in. Startled, Rachel looked at me with a peculiar, guilty expression. "Oh, hi, Amy. What's that on your head?"

"Brainmuff, I'm cold," I lied. Then, naturally as could be, I lied some more. "I don't need any help with it, thanks."

The moorim purred. Clearly I was far gone: I couldn't tell the truth now even if I was willing to pay the moorim's price of lacerated hair.

"No kidding," Rachel said, grinning a little sickly. What was wrong with her? Warily she added, "How'd you find me, anyhow?"

I shrugged, putting off the next mess of lies my mouth seemed bound to utter. I couldn't tell her about the moorim or the prophecy, not here anyway.

Rachel turned away nervously and picked up a Raggedy Anne doll from a hill of similar horrors. "Ugly thing," she said scornfully. Appearance was a big thing with Rachel.

The Jungle lady laughed a merry, sales-making laugh and kept on working over her papers with a pencil with a small plastic cow stuck on the eraser end. The cow probably *was* an eraser. She said, "Take one for yourself. If you buy two, I can give you a break on the price."

"No thanks," Rachel said, suddenly talking loudly and shooting me a defiant look. "It's not my style, and my friend needs every bit of space for her collection as it is. She doesn't go in for duplicates."

Collection? I knew only one person with a stuffed animal collection.

"You're not buying Claudia another stupid stuffed animal?" I protested. "She's drowning in the things already." The moorim moved restlessly in my hair. I wanted to bash the little beast, and Rachel too. Why was *my* best friend getting a present for *Claudia?*

Rachel avoided my eyes. "Yeah, I am, actually. She'd like something small and furry right now because of her Mom and all. She knows these things are pretty babyish, but she likes the comfort."

I was staggered by the idea of Rachel having heart-to-heart talks with Claudia, as well as—*instead of*—with me. It was more than I could deal with right then, things being as they were, so I decided to change the subject. Surely once Rachel knew about the mess I was in, she would turn back into my good, true, best-in-the-world old friend and let Claudia the Ditz buy her own toys.

But how could I explain if I couldn't talk straight?

I fished a piece of paper out of my bag—an old receipt from Cannibal's, as it happened, which gave me a confusing pang of memory, a flash of Cousin Shelly's bright, expectant face—and tried writing on the back, hiding the words from the moorim with my hand as best I could.

I wrote, "Weird news, but first I need help getting this thing off my head."

That's what I thought I wrote, anyway.

I held out the note. Rachel took it.

"Well, this is a comical message," Rachel drawled, holding up the receipt from Cannibal's. " 'Don't come around me anymore,' " she read out loud, slowly and distinctly. " 'You have nothing to do with Kevin, so don't try to horn in.' You came here to give me this?" She glared at me.

I shook my head violently. The moorim fastened itself more firmly, using its teeth as well as all four paws.

"Ooog," I said, and being afflicted with lies I added, "that sure feels good." I began to panic.

"Excuse me, girls," the Jungle lady said, staring at my head. "Could you tell me where you got that little stuffed animal? What's it supposed to be, exactly?"

"It's a Cambodian charivari," I burbled, "from Cuddly Cousins on Madison."

Rachel tossed her hair and and folded her arms, like an impatient palomino pony fretting to gallop away. "Amy," she said, "you are talking crazy and acting totally weird. What's wrong with you?"

"I'm fine," I lied. "Anyway I wouldn't come to you for help if something was wrong." Terrible, terrible, nothing true came out of my mouth. Couldn't Rachel read desperation in my expression or hear it in my voice? Why didn't she want to understand?

Still staring haughtily at me, she said to the Jungle lady, "I'll take an aardvark, in turquoise, gift-wrapped, please."

I stood there mute and miserable while my ex-best friend watched a blue aardvaark get wrapped. Minutes later she walked out without a backward look, swinging a pink plastic shopping bag printed with pictures of velvet palm trees.

The Jungle lady cleared her throat. "When I was a girl, there was nobody I had such awful fights with as my best friend."

Tears were sliding down my cheeks.

The lady added, "And I think you should take that stuffy back where you bought it. There isn't nearly enough filling in it. It flops around every time you move."

She must have been very nearsighted. The moorim had begun drumming all four paws on my skull, like one of Rachel's little brothers having a tantrum. I mumbled something untrue and left the store. Rachel was not in sight. I swallowed my hurt feelings and hurried to where she must be headed: Claudia's.

>—◆—◄

I'd been to Claudia's house twice before. It gave me the creeps. The apartment walls were practically papered with family photos. Even Claudia didn't know who they all were. Some of them still lived in Italy. The pictures turned the apartment into a dark European home brooded over by generations of ancestors.

Claudia's aunt answered the door. She was a thin, nervous lady with dark skin around her eyes as if she never slept. She gave me a once-over you would expect from a sentry at a government installation, then yelled for Claudia, saying her name the Italian way that made it sound like "Cloud-ia."

Claudia came padding down the hallway that was lined with faded faces in wooden frames.

"Oh, hi, Amy," she said in that spacy way of hers. She had on loud bike tights and a huge, tummy-hiding sweatshirt, and she wore her hair down in a dark curtain to her shoulders in an attempt to make her face look thinner, which it didn't. "Want some popcorn? Rachel and me just made a bagful."

She undulated down the hall ahead of me. Claudia had this gliding walk, with her hips leading and her shoulders sort of hunched and drifting after, which looked weird when she was thin. It was kind of impressive when she carried more weight.

Her aunt yelled something after her about posture. I've heard this before at Claudia's. In Italy girls are taught to walk and sit up straight, instead of slouching or leaning on the furniture. The point seems to be slow torture.

In her room, Claudia flopped down on the floor on her stomach with her head propped on her hands so she could see the TV. The floor was covered in thick, green shag carpeting, and there were travel posters all over the walls. The TV sound was low, continuous bop-and-scream. A messy little vanity table stood by the window, covered with a litter of makeup junk. Lined up against the pillows on her bed was a row of stuffed animals wearing dresses, aprons, overalls— clothes she had made for them, all frilly and silly.

It was a little girl's room.

Rachel sat cross-legged on the floor flipping through a comic book. She didn't look at me.

I sat down at the vanity. "Hi, Rachel," I said, and stopped. Now what? Stalemate.

Claudia's eyes snapped wide open. "A RAT! There's a *rat* in your hair!"

Suddenly the little weight lifted off my head. The moorim hopped down onto the vanity table, making neat footprints in the face powder Claudia had spilled on the glass top. Claudia screamed again as the moorim scampered across the floor and stood on its hind legs by the bed, whiskers twitching. It seemed to be checking out the glassy-eyed bears, lions, lizards, even a moose, that shared the pillows.

Claudia hugged her knees and stared with bulging eyes. "I—hate—RATS!"

"That's no rat," Rachel said, frowning at the moorim. "The legs are too long."

"Like," Claudia gasped, "like a WEASEL! I HATE WEA-SELS!"

The moorim sprang up onto the bed, nuzzled itself quickly inside Claudia's PetPurse, and disappeared except for two slim paws hanging out right by the zipper-pull.

"What's it doing?" squealed Claudia. "What's it doing in MY PURSE?"

"It's a moorim, from Kevin's Fayre Farre," I said, "and I think it's sleeping. I hear snores."

"In MY PURSE?"

I collapsed onto the floor, wildly relieved to be rid of the warm little weight on my head and free to speak the truth. "Rachel," I said, "will you listen to me? That wasn't me talking in the Plush Jungle."

"Funny," she said, tossing her hair. "It sounded like you

and it looked like you, and I could have sworn it was you, Amy. You've been so weird since that funeral—"

"Well, my cousin—"

"I don't want to hear any more about your cousin!" she said. "You can't go around fixated on a dead person forever, you know? I don't know how to talk to you anymore. I thought you'd finally lost it for good right there in that lady's store. It was very embarrassing."

"I'm telling you," I said, "that was the moorim controlling what I said!"

"The moorim." Rachel cocked a skeptical, plucked eyebrow. She reached up to poke one of the moorim's paws with one finger. The paw twitched and was withdrawn into the dog-purse. "So this is a creature from Kevin Somebody's fantasy world, and it's followed you home into reality? That's a lot to swallow, Amy."

"If it's not a weasel, it's a RAT," moaned Claudia, hugging her legs tight to her as if afraid the moorim would bite off her toes if she left them exposed. "I can never use that purse AGAIN."

"Well, it's a very special rat, then," I said. "For one thing, it was the moorim that convinced the Branglefolk to give us the prophecy, and for another—"

"It talks?" Rachel said, rolling her eyes.

"Well, not to me," I said. "Only to the Branglefolk, I think, and maybe only in prophecies, not conversations. Now listen, will you? This concerns both of you, too, believe it or not; at least I think it does."

Claudia watched her purse, which didn't move except for the very faint rise and fall that showed the moorim was asleep rather than dead, while I told them both all about my adventures in the Brangle. Rachel ate popcorn from a blue plastic bowl, one piece at a time, pretending not to listen. I couldn't figure out why she was acting so unfriendly.

Claudia looked from her purse to me and back again. "Wow!" she said.

Wow. What a fabulous, articulate response! All the tension went out of me. I suddenly wanted to do nothing but sleep. Maybe when I woke up Rachel would be my best friend again, and Claudia would talk sense. What kind of a princess was Claudia the Ditz going to make in the Fayre Farre, for goodness' sake?

Rachel frowned. "So how does this prophecy go, exactly?" She sounded sarcastic, but she was interested, all right.

"I don't know," I admitted. "I can only remember bits and snatches. Well, it was *long*—"

"What's it doing now?" Claudia interrupted feverishly. "What's it doing in there in my PURSE? It's making a noise, don't you hear that?"

We listened. The moorim was certainly making a noise; a noise I recognized. It was singing the tune that went with the words of the prophecy.

I went over and lay down on the bed, putting my head close to the PursePet. The faint, wavery sound rang in my head. So did Claudia's little screams of horror, and her helpful warning, "Amy, look out, what if it bites YOUR FACE OFF?"

"You come listen," I said, motioning Claudia over next to me. "It's in your purse, Claudia, and it sounds like—I can almost hear words—"

Claudia, her dark eyes wide, crawled onto the bed and put her head very nervously near the purse. She jumped, looking stunned. Then she shut her eyes, licked her lips, and began to sing in a very wavery, scratchy voice—the words of the prophecy:

"A princess in mourning, a princess in gold,
A princess with talents as yet to unfold,
Shall join with the strength of the hero foretold,
And win, if their hearts be both tender and bold.
One princess must press on through terrors and fears
And solve the great riddle of using the years.
One princess must choose for a guide and a friend
A being she fears but will love in the end.
One princess must bring from her distant home's heart
A magic more mighty than any smith's art.
These three, imprisoned in walls made of stone,
Pressed to the uttermost, bounded by bone,
Using a weapon they already own,
Can bring the prince worthily home to his throne."

Claudia finished in a small voice, "Are you sure any of this is about me? I'm not brave."

Rachel ripped a sheet of notebook paper from a pad on Claudia's bureau, and then motioned to Claudia to sing it all again, which she did—three times, one for each of us, I guess—while Rachel scribbled down the words with a chewed-up pencil stub from her pocket.

"Well, I got it all, I think," she said, chomping nervously on the pencil as she read and re-read her transcription. "Boy. Is this for real?"

But she knew as well as I did that Claudia couldn't have made up that poem.

Somehow their getting the prophecy seemed to let me off the hook for a while. The two of them could go fix things for Rotten Kevin. I was a princess in mourning; I wasn't supposed to be wrestling with moorims for truth. I was supposed to be back home giving visitors coffee and listening to them

106

tell me how wonderful Cousin Shelly had been. Rolling off Claudia's bed, I stretched out on the floor.

"Amy, when do you have to get this magic sword to Kevin?" Rachel asked.

I tried to work it out. My brain drowsed. Maybe when the moorim slept I had to sleep, too? Or maybe I had just not had enough sleep back in the Brangle to hold me.

"Come on, Amy," Rachel coaxed. "I'm sorry I was snippy with you."

"Sure." I yawned. "Kevin just said he needs the sword soon. Listen, I have to lie down."

"You are lying down," Claudia said. She took the sheet of paper from Rachel and studied it.

I curled up on the floor and dozed, but I could hear the two of them talking over the garble from Claudia's TV.

Claudia: "Let's finish the popcorn. We don't want to go to Kevin's country on an empty stomach."

Rachel: "I thought you weren't brave enough to go."

I heard getting-up sounds. I was so surprised I almost woke up.

"It doesn't say here that anybody dies," Claudia said. "And I want to meet this Kevin. Isn't it romantic, having a boy pop into Amy's life from the past like that?"

Romantic! Kevin and me! I snorted sarcastically, or thought I did.

The floor under my cheek vibrated slightly as Rachel paced. The rug under my nose smelled faintly of butter. Claudia did too much eating in her room.

"The timing is *terrible*," Rachel said and thumped or kicked a piece of furniture. She got physical sometimes when she was upset. "We've got major reports and exams before spring break, you know? You'd think Amy could be more *considerate*."

Claudia said, "You don't have to come with me."

"Who says you're going anywhere? Amy has the only key to the place, that pin of hers. Are you going to take it?"

"Rachel Breakstone, I am not a *stealer*," Claudia said. "I have my own way into the Fayre Farre. The moorim will take me."

"The moorim is Amy's, too." Now Rachel sounded snippy with Claudia. And she said *I* acted weird!

Claudia said, "Well, it's in *my* purse. I'll walk the purse through one of the park arches with the moorim inside it. Bet that will work, and I won't even have to touch the icky little rat-thing. Don't you want to meet this Kevin? Not everybody gets to meet a prince."

"If you're going, I'll go too," Rachel said with an exasperated sigh. "Listen, let me borrow this scarf for the trip, okay? It might be cold and windy at the Fayre Farre. If there's anything I hate, it's going someplace where my hair whips all over and gets in my eyes."

I turned over on the floor because my left knee was hurting from leaning on it too long.

I thought I heard Rachel say, "Are you sure about this, Claudia? It could be dangerous," and Claudia say, "It can't be any worse than writing my report about the Haymarket Riots for Mr. Kaplan."

When I woke up, the room was empty, the TV was off. Zia Cynzia, in the doorway, said, "Your mother knows you sleeping here tonight?"

I got up from the floor. "Where are Rachel and Claudia?"

"Gone to the movies," Zia Cynzia said. "What they told me. Claudia's mother want me to look after her." She gazed somberly at me.

I looked away.

She sighed hugely. "Don't worry your mother like Claudia worry me, okay?"

On Claudia's bed, the lineup of stuffed animals faced me: the aardvark, a pair of floppy-nosed zebras, a very beat-up looking monkey—no purse in the form of a stuffed dog.

And no moorim on my head, either. I was really free.

I phoned Mom and told her I was on my way home.

TEN

Truth and Tomato Juice

WALKING DOWN THIRD AVENUE in the chilly evening with a million other people, I felt very confused. Rachel and Claudia had abandoned me and run off with my adventure, but I had let them go without a murmur. It had even seemed right, somehow, for them to go ahead without me. Was I losing my mind over all this?

Well, what had I thought would happen?

I'd thought we would figure out the prophecy and all go together into Kevin's magic world, sort of Three Musketeers, since Claudia was apparently included whether I liked it or not. We'd be strong enough, the three of us, to make things come out all right even if we had to fight with Kevin—Prince Kavian himself—to do it.

Not that I'd thought out any of this beforehand. No, brilliant old Amy only caught on when it was too late, and everybody had abandoned her to go gallivanting off on their own to *her* magic place that *she* had been invited into by its creator because of a childhood *she* shared with him. Well, that's pushing it, but you get the idea.

Maybe the moorim wouldn't actually take them through to the Fayre Farre. But it seemed to me that the moorim had invited them in by singing the prophecy. So I had been used as some kind of pack-mule, carrying the moorim from the Fayre Farre to Claudia's apartment so that the creature could take the other two, the really important princesses, back to do their stuff in Kevin's story.

Feeling betrayed, I stumped along with my hands in my pockets and my head down, making everybody else walk around me.

So my job now was just to toddle off and fetch Kevin's magic sword, lug it back into the Fayre Farre, and give it to him. Well, nuts to that. Let him send one of his other precious princesses for it. He was only Rotten Kevin the Corner Kid. He didn't deserve three whole princesses running errands for him.

>—◆—◀

It was after nine when I got home. The apartment was quiet and dark and smelled of food, and it seemed . . .

crowded? I turned on the living-room light. There were a dozen houseplants from Shelly's apartment lined up on the windowsill. My eyes watered.

"Amy?" Mom's voice, from the kitchen.

My parents were sitting at the table in there, surrounded by stacked, racked, freshly washed dishes. They both looked beat, but relieved. The shiva was finally over.

All I could think of was how hungry I was, having missed dinner completely. On the table between my parents sat half a loaf of rye bread, a knife, and the butter dish. I sat down and cut myself some bread.

Dad leaned back, rubbing his eyes. "I'm glad tonight was the end of it," he said. "With all the things people said about Shelly, all the memories, I started missing her worse than before."

And I, of course, had missed it all because I'd been in the Fayre Farre, or sleeping. It seemed to me that I had barely thought of Shelly, really, in—days? Or was it only hours? Kevin and his world were distracting me from what really mattered.

Nobody noticed my hot, flushed face. Dad hadn't even been talking to me; his sad smile at Mom told me who he was really talking to. And Mom wasn't really looking at me. She was looking at my head, and she sort of relaxed all over when she saw that the moorim was gone.

I ripped the center out of the bread chunk I'd cut and began slathering butter on the crust. This was all I was good for, while thin, pretty, fake-best-friend Rachel and Claudia the Ditz waltzed off to play princesses for Kevin.

Mom said, "We've all been missing Shell. Amy most of all, maybe."

"I just think it's so incredibly stupid and unfair that she

died," I said. God, it felt great to say what I felt straight out and true, with no moorim monitoring me.

Mom sighed, "I think so, too." She dabbed at her eyes with a paper napkin.

"Everybody has to come to terms with it their own way," Dad said.

I snarled, around a mouthful of bread, "I don't want to come to terms with it. Everybody does everything they can to forget that a person died, and then they say they've 'come to terms with it.' I think that's disgusting."

"It's not forgetting," Dad began, looking pained.

"So," Mom said, leaning forward with her elbows on the table, "what should we be doing instead?"

"Anything to hang onto them," I said. "Not let death have them." I thought of Sebbian, and of the Bone Men. "I mean— suppose you could bring somebody back? Or go after them at least partway for a while, so you wouldn't have to feel so left behind?"

Dad said quietly, "Shelly didn't die on purpose, bunny-hunch. No use being angry with her."

"I know," I muttered, and tore into the bread again. "I never said she did; I'm not stupid, Dad. But I miss her. I don't have to go to her apartment or listen to people reminiscing about her to miss her, you know. There are things I'd like to talk about with her."

"You know you can always—" Dad began, but Mom shook her head, and he stopped.

"It's not the same, Dad," I said, "talking to you on the telephone in Los Angeles."

Dad looked down at his plate with the crumbs on it and didn't say anything, and I felt truly horrible.

"Of course," I hurried on, babbling insanely, "you being

far away isn't the same as Shelly being dead, I'm not saying that. Only there are some similarities, that's all." Worse and worse. Where was I?—and where had I been when I started this awful conversation?

Dad got up. "I've got some work to do," he said. "See you later, Sarah. Amy—" He looked at me. "I don't know what else I can say to you about all this."

He walked out of the kitchen.

"That wasn't very nice of you," Mom said. "He's really sad and tired, Amy. We all are."

Well, I could have reminded her that she was the one who was always worrying out loud about California, so who was she to tell me I wasn't being considerate of Dad's feelings?

"I think you're more upset about Shelly than I've realized, Amy. I'm sorry." She got up and stretched wearily, smiling a self-mocking smile. "I haven't been very grown-up about it all, I guess."

Oh no, I thought, *not a heart-to-heart*—nothing was harder to take. I went to work on more of the bread, thinking longingly about a story Dad had told once about how Marlon Brando stuffed bread in his ears so he could sleep in a noisy motel room. I really would have liked to have stuffed bread in my ears to shut out what Mom was saying.

Of course the point of the story was that Marlon Brando hadn't been able to get the bread out of his ears the next morning and had to be taken to the doctor's.

"On top of everything else, I'm scared to death of this move," Mom said, keeping her voice down. "We mean to come back when we can, but I know people who've gone to Los Angeles with the same plan and never come back. They live forever in a place they hate!"

"So why are we going?" I said.

Mom walked over to the window above the sink and looked out, so at least her back was to me.

"Your father's not sure it's right, either," she said. "I should be helping him think it out so it *will* work. And it can work, of course it can—we're not Silly Putty, we're smart, able people. I can find some kind of work out there. I've even put some feelers out." She walked over and patted my hair. "And you'll make new friends."

"I like my old friends," I said.

"Will you write to Rachel?" she asked.

"No," I said angrily. What a dumb idea! Especially now. "We're hardly friends anymore anyhow. I won't even miss her."

Her hand hovered. I ducked my head away.

"You should be happy about that," I said. "You've never liked Rachel."

"Huh," Mom said, plumping down in her chair again. "I can't say that I do, actually. I'm glad you've enjoyed her friendship, but I can't approve wholeheartedly of a kid who says she's going to change her name from Rachel to Raquel as soon as she gets her nose done. Are you planning to finish that whole stick of butter tonight?"

I shoved back from the table. *"What?"* I said, meaning about Rachel, not the butter.

"Oh, it's not her fault," Mom said. "Her parents started it, changing from Beckstein to Breakstone. Breakstone. I ask you! Is that New England Gothic, or what?" She grinned, a real big grin, for the first time since Shelly's death.

"You sound like Uncle Irv," I said. "Or Aunt Jennie. What's the big deal? This is America, lots of people change their names. You can be what you want to be here, that's the whole idea."

Mom cocked her head and considered me gravely, and the panicky tightness in my chest went away. We had somehow moved off the dangerous ground of grieving and feelings. We were into that place where she and I had always been able to talk comfortably.

"Sure," she said, "but it's a struggle, Amy, not a casual, routine sort of thing. Shelly told me once she thought that was *the* American puzzle: how to deal with your forebears and their values. Not that it's an original idea, but you know, doing social work she had a lot of contact with the newer waves of immigrants, so it was always right there in front of her."

"What was?" I asked. Shelly hadn't talked much with me about her work. I always thought of her as somebody who took me to the movies, or to the Botanical Gardens in Brooklyn or the little Conservatory Garden up at the north end of Central Park where we sometimes had had picnics on the weekends.

"What was what?" Mom focused on me again. She'd kind of lost it there for a minute. "Oh—what Shelly said. She said that in the old country, whatever that country was, people were defined by where they and their families had lived for generations, and they expected to go on living there pretty much the same way, as the same kind of people. Once you uproot and come to America where everybody moves around all the time, then all of a sudden your identity isn't automatic anymore. All of a sudden you have to think about it and choose it for yourself."

"By changing from Beckstein to Breakstone?" I said.

Mom said, "That's what you can do in this country: dump your whole past, or try to. No wonder our best books and plays are all about families, parents and kids, ethnic roots. Always chewing it over, doing it over, working it out. Except it never does work out. It just keeps weaving along."

A startling idea hit me. Maybe Rachel would celebrate getting her nose done, when it happened, by changing not only her name but her actual religion. Maybe she was hanging out with Claudia to learn how to be a Catholic.

"Tell you one thing," Mom said. "If Rachel does become Raquel, the chances are even that her kids will turn around and decide to be more orthodox than your Uncle Irving's rabbi."

"Why?" I asked, baffled.

"Just remember," she said, "you heard it from me first. She'll name her son Jason, and he'll change it to Joshua and grow earlocks."

Another boy I knew had changed his name: from Kevin the Corner Kid to Kavian Prince, the Promised Champion. I wondered what Mom would make of that.

I said, "Do you remember Kevin Malone?"

"Of course I do." Mom looked surprised. "That poor kid— no wonder he was wild, with that family of his. What made you think of him? I thought you'd repressed your memories of him completely."

"I didn't expect *you* to remember."

"Sweetheart," she said, "I have a reason to remember; not a good reason, I'm afraid. Open the fridge, will you? I'm dying for something cool to drink."

We split a big can of tomato juice with a slice of lime in each glass. Across the courtyard a neighbor's TV sent out flickering blue light, like foggy signals from another world.

Mom said, "Remember when I went down to the corner houses to complain about Kevin stealing from you?"

"Sure," I said. "It was great. You said, 'I am going to go talk to those people,' and you did it, and nothing bad happened. It worked."

Mom looked unhappy. "It worked all right, but something bad did happen. I just didn't think you needed to know about it. Shelly came across the case records a few years ago. She told me about it. Kevin showed up at a hospital that same night with a broken arm and two cracked ribs. Not long afterward he ran away for the first time. Then, later, he was actually taken out of his home."

"Taken?" I was intrigued. "I thought he was arrested and locked up in juvenile jail, that was what everybody said. And nobody was sorry, either, none of the kids in our building anyway."

Mom jiggled the lime slice around in her juice glass. "He was locked up, but that came later. His first disappearances were to foster homes. Those broken bones weren't the first or the last his father gave him."

I shook my head, thinking about Kevin keeping my pin to commemorate a day when his father hadn't beaten him up. "I never suspected, back then."

"It's not the kind of thing people talk about with their kids," she said, "a drunk who beats up his wife and his children."

"The mother, too?"

"That's what Shell said."

I thought about Dad, working on script pages in bed, arranging his ticket back to Los Angeles on the phone. I thought about not having a father around much, versus having one around all the time who hit you. I felt almost ashamed of my good luck when somebody else had had such bad luck. Even Rotten Kevin.

Rotten Kevin, who might hold a heck of a grudge, I suddenly realized. Kevin's father put him in the hospital because I complained to Mom, and Mom complained to Kevin's mother, and Kevin's mother must have said something to Kevin's father. Our prince might have some unpleasant surprises in mind for me in the Fayre Farre.

But no—that didn't make sense. Mom said Kevin's father had been abusing them all along. I hadn't *made* his father beat him up. Now, if Kevin was as logical and smart as I was, and could figure that out . . .

That was when I knew I was going back to the Fayre Farre. To help, I thought. Besides, the place wasn't full of people grieving for Cousin Shell or worrying about moving to California or loading their feelings onto me.

"Boy, it's late," I said.

Mom agreed. She pointed out that I had school tomorrow, and she had two buyers coming in early, so it was off to bed with both of us.

With one of us, actually. But she didn't need to know that.

ELEVEN

Passing for Paula

IN MY ROOM, I brushed my hair out in front of the mirror. Not smooth blonde hair like Rachel's or slick black hair like Claudia's, but long, thick, kinky brown hair with red highlights, like Cousin Shell's. Only on her it had looked really good.

On me—

Anyway, where I was going I was a princess in mourning, and I wanted to look nice, if not royal.

I knew what I wanted to wear on this trip into the Fayre Farre—my last, maybe. Good pants, a silky cotton T-shirt under a soft corduroy shirt with a pretty floral print, running shoes, and my wine-colored windbreaker with lots of pockets with velcro closures. I was risking the ruin of some more of my favorite clothes, but Kevin had looked really good the last time I'd met him in the Fayre Farre, and Rachel always looked super.

No pack, though I considered taking my small one: I didn't mean to stay away long enough to need it.

And the rhinestone rose, pinned to my collar, of course.

I wrote a note for my parents ("Gone to do some thinking, sorry if I've been awful lately—don't worry, I'm safe and sound, home soon, love Amy") and left it on my pillow. With any luck, I'd be back before morning and they would never know I'd gone.

I tiptoed down the hall, let myself out the side door, and ran down the fire stairs—fifteen flights to the lobby—and out.

Breathless and tingly—what if the doorman had seen me? What if he called Mom up on the house phone?—I took buses uptown and then across the park, and then walked quickly up Central Park West toward my old block.

It felt sort of exciting, to be going—well, home, in a way—back to the place I had lived as a little girl, in the days when I didn't know anything about Kevin's family. A family that Cousin Shelly would have described as dysfunctional. Now I had an idea what that actually meant.

My old street was so changed, it added to my sense of eons of time having passed since those days. New trees had been planted in the dirt squares along the edge of the sidewalk. Everything was so neat: the lids chained to the garbage cans, the curbs painted with thick enamel for fire zones and loading zones and the bus stop at the corner.

Lights glowed in the curtained bow windows on the third floor of Kevin's old building. The rest were dark. I realized that I had never known just what floor his family had lived on.

I walked up the steep stairs and into the little vestibule of Kevin's brownstone. As I had expected, the inner door was locked. Sometimes if you punch the downstairs call buttons and jabber in a high voice into the speaker grille, somebody will buzz you in. But then when you don't show up at their apartment they know somebody's wandering around in the building. After dark people get extra nervous about that.

So I unpinned the rhinestone rose and waggled the sharp end in the keyhole of the inner door, meanwhile shutting my eyes hard and visualizing the little stones glowing with LOCK-OPENING POWER from the Fayre Farre.

The door swung open and a creaky voice said, "What's the matter, Paula, forget your keys again?"

I jerked back the pin and hid it in my pocket.

A tiny, withered old man stood there squinting at me through milky-looking eyes. He had red pinch marks from glasses on the bridge of his bony nose, but luckily for me the glasses were not on the scene just then.

"Well?" he said. "I can't be jumping up and down all the time just to let you in, you know."

I nodded enthusiastically. "Mmmf, mmm, 'anks," I said, trying to sound like a Paula and quickly sidling past him.

"Just as long as you didn't leave those keys laying on the bakery counter again, like you did the last time," he said, carefully shutting the door behind us. "Got no time or money to change the locks again, you hear me?"

"Mmmf," I said, heading for the elevator.

He shook his head and hobbled away into the front ground-floor apartment.

I got into the elevator and pressed B, for basement. The sword was buried treasure, sort of, and where else could you bury something in a New York building?

Kevin's basement was changed beyond recognition.

I'd been in there once, on a dare from one of the kids in my own building. That one visit had made me briefly famous and admired among my friends.

I remembered the place well: bare cement walls, shiny black leakage gleaming on the cracked floor all the way from the jammed storage room to the dirty hole that housed the furnace and the boiler. A stained mattress had been propped against one wall; I had seen a rat scuttle up over a crazy stack of crates and dive into a hole in that mattress.

Not to mention the smell, mostly old cooking and stale beer.

Now it smelled of furnace heat and dusty water pipes, and the walls were painted lavender and blue. The boiler room and the storage space both had metal doors with locks. Where the mattress had leaned stood a washer and dryer and a deep white sink with a mop draining in it. The floor was surfaced with green tile.

The passage to the back, once dark and packed with bundles that might have been garbage or people's belongings, was now lit by a wire-caged bulb and lined with neat plastic trash cans.

I held up the rose pin. It glowed faintly when I turned it toward the sink.

I went over for a closer look. The sink was not very promising as a hiding place. It looked as if it got a lot of use. Users would find anything hidden there, wouldn't they?

But where would you hide something in a sink anyway?

Down—the pin's beam indicated—underneath.

I hunkered down to see if anything was taped to the underside. There was nothing, only the pipes, and the wall behind them which the painters had not bothered with since you couldn't see it unless you were down where I was. In fact, there wasn't even a plaster coating here, like on the wall above. I could see a few dark red bricks, set unevenly with pale crusts of mortar squeezed out along the seams.

I turned the faint beam of the rhinestones—were they really shining, or was I imagining it?—toward the wall. I moved the brooch back and forth slowly. Water dripped monotonously into the sink above my head.

One of the bricks took on the glow of the magic light: special effects in Kevin's old basement! Gingerly I ran my hand along the edge of the brick. Crumbly mortar fell away onto the floor. The brick rocked slightly when I pressed it.

My heart was bumping along: I didn't much like the idea of feeling around in some dank, black space for a sharp-edged weapon. Never mind the possibility of giant waterbugs. Was this the place? You couldn't fit a whole sword into the length of a brick, so maybe the blade had a detachable handle? Humble guise, Kevin had said—a folding umbrella? Too big.

Behind me the elevator descended with a whine of machinery. It stopped on the ground floor and stayed there, and then up it went again.

I dropped the rose pin back in my jacket pocket and pressed the velcro shut. Then I scrunched down by the wall and eased the brick out by sheer friction with my fingertips. It came with a grating sound, and it was so much heavier than I'd expected that I almost dropped it. I leaned it on end against the wall.

There in the back of the cavity, in plain view, was what had to be Kevin's magical Farsword. It was a little package no longer than my middle finger, all wrapped up in discolored white cotton cloth and tied around and around with a piece of green plastic lanyard.

I stared, itching with curiosity but scared, too. The stained cloth reminded me of, well, mummy wrappings, and isn't treasure always booby-trapped against robbers? Trust Kevin to forget to mention the ax blade that would drop out of the ceiling and chop my head off when I released the secret lever by removing the package.

I grabbed it. Nothing awful happened. I eased a loop of the ancient lanyard around the end of the little bundle, and then the whole thing came loose.

Folded up inside was a familiar shape: a red-handled Swiss Army knife.

I laughed. The great Farsword!

It wasn't even one of the fancy models, loaded with options so when you open everything out it looks like a mechanical porcupine. There were just two blades. Somebody had scratched a name—"Dan"—on the plastic grip on one side and rubbed in ink to make the letters show.

Poor Dan. I wondered who he'd been, and how his knife had fallen into Kevin's grubby paws. Kevin had been lucky, for once. The only thing that hadn't been changed down here was probably this old-fashioned slop sink, previously hidden behind a mattress. So nobody had found his treasure hole.

Relieved that I wasn't going to have to smuggle a giant sword into the Fayre Farre past all kinds of Famishers and whatnot, I wrapped the knife up again, stuffed it into another of my jacket pockets, and tried to replace the brick in its niche. It was a tight fit. I had to keep the brick level and straight to push it in all the way.

"What are you doing down here all this time?" quavered a voice. "You're not Paula!"

It was the old man, and he had his glasses on. He glared at me from the bottom flight of the fire stairs, clutching the rail with his knobby hands.

I jumped up. "Someone I know used to live here. I came to find something for him that he left," I said. I was still a little high on being able to tell the truth without a moorim chomping on my head. Besides, maybe the old man would understand. Maybe he was psychic or fey or something.

"You'll find the police, that's what you'll find!" he cried shrilly. "I've already called them."

I bolted for the door to the delivery alley. It opened easily when I hit it with my shoulder, but set off a terrific clanging alarm. Over the noise I could hear the old man yelling, "I knew you weren't Paula, you didn't fool me!"

I ran up the block, digging the pin out of my pocket again. The little stones glowed when I turned the pin southward on Central Park West. So I trotted downtown along the dark wall edging the park, holding the pin in one hand and clutching the wrapped knife in my pocket with the other.

Nobody bothered me. Maybe nobody saw me at all. Maybe the pin and the knife, between them, protected me from cops, loungers, dealers, muggers, and the regular people strolling on Central Park West on a mild spring night.

Cheery little lights were strung in the trees around the Tavern-on-the-Green just inside the park at Sixty-sixth Street. The restaurant, a pretty brick cottage with tall glass windows bowed out like the panes of a greenhouse, was always packed with people. Inside I saw waiters hovering over tables crowded with diners, the tiny bulbs of the chandeliers gleaming above them all. Outside, the fat white globes of the tall lamps on the terraces shed a cool glow over white cast-iron tables and chairs.

The pull of the pin was now almost physical. It drew me past the restaurant on a looping pathway. I paused to catch my breath and to take a long last look at all those lights.

Then I hurried along the path over the traffic-roaring Sixty-sixth Street transverse. I ran down a steep slope, to an arch that had no name on any map. It was a simple stone bridge carrying a footpath into the park at a place where the park itself lies much lower than street level.

No telling who or what I would find waiting for me on the other side of this arch, I thought. I tucked the rose pin back into my pocket and sealed it in.

Time to go.

But I hesitated, listening to the traffic roar along the park wall and to the silence inside the arch over the coal black bridle path.

Suddenly I was deathly scared, for a city kid's normal reasons: somebody of my own world—some thief or mugger or unwelcoming street person—might be lurking inside that archway. With the glowing pin tucked away in one pocket and the wrapped "sword" in the other, I felt charged with energy, but something in the real world might keep me from bringing Kevin what I had found.

Well, if I just stood there, something certainly would— my own panic if nothing else! I walked forward with the biggest, most confident stride I could muster, caught my foot on something, and stumbled against the broken drinking fountain by the arch.

I more or less fell through the cold, dividing curtain of air into Kevin's country.

TWELVE

The Rose Traveler

BEHIND ME water splashed. Turning, I saw a sparkling fountain shaped like a fish jumping in a stone basin, in place of the drinking fountain.

Here, it was just dusk. On a gentle slope up ahead of me a crowd of people carried flickering lights. Horns hooted mournfully in the background. No doubt about it, I was once again in the Fayre Farre breathing Kevin's air, feeling the stir of the sunset breezes of his world. My heart thudded.

With quiet movement all around me, I walked forward into a broad meadow.

Up ahead where the moving lights led, a mansion crowned a slight rise in the land. Long flags, streamers really, flew from its towers. It wasn't hard to recognize the roofline of the Tavern-on-the-Green, but with all its pointed gables multiplied and enlarged.

A figure in a swirly dress brushed by me, stopped, and pointed at me. "The Rose Traveler!" she cried in a sort of trilling whoop. "See, the Rose Traveler!"

I looked down and saw the faint glow of the rhinestones shining right through the fabric of my jacket pocket. I tore the pocket open and put my hand inside to hide the glow with my fingers.

Way too late; strangers closed around me in a dense pattern of moving lights and thin trails of smoke. They were all young looking, slim, and dressed in odd costumes—snug vests over full-sleeved shirts, tight pants and boots or skirts ending in artful tatters—in shades of gold and green. There was a strong piney scent in the air, as if all these people wore tree sap for perfume.

I had a moment of panic as they pressed in around me and more or less carried me with them, singing a song full of slip-sliding harmonies. There was a wild gleaming about them, where the candlelight touched their singing mouths and their flashing, almond-shaped eyes, that made me think of something not human—wonderful androids, maybe, every one of them beautiful, sparkling, and creepily unreal.

I almost longed for the dusty Branglefolk.

And yet I felt a deep, hungry feeling pulling at my heart, drawing me toward this part of the Fayre Farre—the graceful, dusky beauty of it. I was glad to have the solidity of the rose pin in one pocket and the weight of Kevin's knife in another to hold me down to earth and remind me of what I was doing here.

I turned to the person nearest me and asked casually, "Is Kevin here?"

She shook her head. "Kavian Prince is awaited."

Oh, boy, I had hit the language thing at last. That made me feel more solidly surrounded by Kevin's world than anything else.

"I'm also looking for two girls," I added, "one black-haired and chubby and one with long blonde hair?"

"No one gathers at Elf Home but elvenfolk," she said, tossing her head with haughty amusement.

Elves! Now I saw the pattern: these almond-eyed folk were Kevin's elves, the Branglemen were his version of dwarves, and the Famishers were his horrible monsters. Somewhere there were trolls and giants, too, in whatever form his imagination had cast them. I was doing okay tonight, so far: better elves than trolls.

I hoped Rachel and Claudia were doing well, wherever they were. What a shock this place must be to them, coming into it for the first time!

If the moorim had gotten them in. I wished I knew where they were, and whether it was actually going to be Two Musketeers and Another Musketeer and Kevin, or just Kevin and me, period, against the White One.

The mansion had a set of tall wooden doors with twisty, vinelike carvings all over them. The doors swung wide open and everybody, with me in the middle, crowded into a hall with a gallery running all around above it. It was nothing like the real Tavern, which is loaded with stained glass, etched mirrors, and wood paneling. They don't do Corner Kids there.

Instead of chandeliers of miniature light bulbs, torches burned. Banks of green branches drooped off the wall sconces and the gallery railing, and pine shavings crunched under foot. It was like a room made of forest.

I found that I was squinting, though the torches didn't seem to be giving off much smoke. The atmosphere was just peculiar, sort of blurry as if with heat-ripples—yet it felt heavy and cold. In the midst of that crowd I was shivering.

Around the edges of the hall I saw tables with circular tops made of woven slats. Some of these tables had been taken apart and the tops stacked by the walls to make space in the middle of the hall where the crowd gathered, as if they had come to dance.

The floor at the back of the hall rose in a sort of mound draped in rugs of live turf, pale green and gold. On top of the mound, on seats cut into live trees growing up into the ceiling, sat two green-skinned people in long robes, with circlets of leaves on their heads like crowns.

The crowd fell back and left me to walk up to the dais on my own. I would have paid money for a glimpse of a familiar face just then—Rachel, Kevin, Claudia, even Singer or Scarface—but there were none.

One of the crowned people stood up as I came near. He—I think it was a he, though the form was straight and sexless as a little child's and the wheat-gold hair hung almost to the waist—lifted his hand in a theatrical gesture that on him looked perfectly natural. The whole feeling was so stagey and pretty—it was like a production of *A Midsummer Night's Dream* I had seen at the theater in the park last summer.

Only this was not theater. It just had some of the same feel. The current of chilliness in the place made my skin prickle. I couldn't wait to get rid of the sword, find the girls if they were around, and get us all out of there.

The standing one spoke to me in a sweet voice. "Is it true that you have the crystal rose?"

Rhinestones at home, crystals here.

They were all staring at me expectantly. Was I supposed to bow or something? I didn't think I could do that convincingly, but better not to be too casual, either. These weren't Shakespeare's elves or Santa's elves, they were Kevin's elves, which meant I'd better watch my step.

"I do carry the rose," I said with as much dignity as I could muster; it felt important to rise to the level that Kevin's imagination had set. "I've come to deliver something to, er, Prince Kavian. Is he among you?" I could see he wasn't, but it seemed polite to ask.

If they did know where to find Kevin, they didn't rush to let me in on the secret. Nobody said a word—no whispers, no elf nudging the elf next to him and asking what did the stranger say, huh, what did she say?

"She traveled also with one of the Oldest," observed the other crowned person after a while, pointing at my head with a wand of what looked like braided straw. She looked female only because of the redness of her lips.

Oldest? Did she mean the moorim? But it was gone, so how could she tell? Did it leave tracks? I resisted an impulse to reach up and pat my hair. *Elves just know stuff, it's how they are,* I told myself.

I brushed my lower left pocket for the reassuring bulk of the knife in there. Could elves lift something from that pocket without the noise of velcro ripping open? Maybe, but the knife was where I'd put it.

I braced my shoulders and went ahead on nerve. It was all I had. "I'd like to make this delivery as soon as I can, being only a visitor here. So if you can tell me where to find Kavian—?"

"He is expected," the Elf King said, and sat down again. Nobody else moved or spoke. They looked at me. So what was I supposed to do now? I cleared my throat. I was thirsty.

"Could somebody tell me when he's supposed to arrive?" I asked. "And there are a couple of other visitors around somewhere, friends of mine—"

The second crowned person laughed, a chilly little clinking sound like what happens when you drop a frying pan into the sink on top of a glass that you didn't notice was in there. "A veritable inrush of outsiders, the omen we have expected. You bring more than the treasure Kavian Prince commissioned you to bring, Rose Traveler."

What did that mean? Before I could even decide to ask, more horns sounded, this time a sort of bugle-call of high, spiky notes that I didn't need to have interpreted. It was an alarm.

"Famishers!" I heard distant shouts. "Famishers are coming!"

The soft-breeze sound in the hall suddenly intensified into a galelike rushing; the elves were laughing. The two crowned ones stood up again. One said, "We will take your burden and complete your errand. Give us Farfarer."

Farfarer? As I stood there, confused, it came to me like a wave breaking: what is always true about magic swords? They have names. What I had in my velcro-sealed pocket was a Swiss Army knife named Farfarer. Oh, brother.

And these green people wanted it.

There must have been more than a hundred elves in the hall, packed into the strange, wavery air and laughing softly like the wind before a storm. They made no threatening moves but watched me with interest.

"Farfarer is for Kavian only," I said as firmly as I could.

"We will see that he gets it," the other crowned person said.

But she wasn't wearing a moorim, was she?

"Give it to us," the Elf King said. "Farfarer brings dangers with it that are alien to you. If we relieve you of this burden, many troubles will be diverted from you and your life will be filled with serenity and joy."

The horn-call warning of the Famishers sounded again, closer. I wavered, twitching and sweating with nerves. Enemies hounded Kevin across his own secret country. The Farsword was his one hope, and I didn't like the way the lady elf had referred to it as "treasure."

"No," I said. "I'll give it to him myself, thanks."

Immediately everybody began moving, like a flickering of leaves blown in a wind and just as hard to follow. You could barely tell one of them from another when they stood still, but now it was like the middle of a windstorm under the park trees in autumn.

The candles went out almost all at once. The torches on the walls streamed and smoked and died. I was left standing in shimmering darkness with the sensation of a huge crowd moving very quickly all around me. Inside, the hollow sound of a cold wind rushed around and around us within the walls of Elf Home.

Outside I could hear the horns howling. Behind that came the high, hungry squeals of the Famishers, closing in. Which way to run in the blackness? Where to hide in this whirlpool of elves?

The gallery, I thought. *You don't know what direction to take, so go* up.

I dashed straight ahead into the darkness. With gusty laughter, forms that I sensed rather than felt seemed to snatch themselves out of the air in front of me just in time to avoid collisions. I almost lost my balance, flinching and swerving, in fear of being hit in passing or being rushed for the Farsword.

In six good strides I felt the rise of the dais under my feet, and then I barked my shin on the edge of one of the twisted-tree thrones. Grabbing the trunk of the thing and bracing the soles of my running shoes on the seat, I did my best to swarm up into the branches.

I thought the tree would take me onto the balcony. Instead I found myself climbing into what felt like long, dry, grassy leaves packed close in layers spreading out from the trunk. Then I was outside on a cold night with a huge moon blazing in the blackness overhead.

My arm muscles burned with the strain of the climb, and my shin ached where I'd hit it on the seat edge. From my perch in the wide, flat spread of branches that roofed the hall, I looked down on the massacre outside the walls.

The moonlight was so bright that the racing figures below cast shadows on the pale grass. What looked like a hundred Famishers galloped around with their tusks flashing and their snaky necks weaving as they snatched at the elves running among them. Over everything blew the chilly breeze of the elves' laughter.

I swear they were laughing even as the round, fanged mouths of the Famishers chomped them like celery. The elves ran like little kids, on their toes. One dodged a Famisher and then somehow, quick as light, swung up on its shaggy back and hung on. I saw a flicker of motion as the elf slung a thin rope across in front of the monster's throat, catching the free end in the other hand and giving a hard twist. The Famisher fell, turning its head back on its snaky neck so its round, toothy mouth could gnash at the elf.

A skirted elf rode a Famisher right below me, and I saw her arms flex hard. Black blood sprayed out from the front of the Famisher's neck where the cord bit, and down the creature went in a tangle of knobby legs. But another running Famisher veered alongside and plucked the elf off with a crunching sound. I covered my ears with my hands.

The elf's face was turned toward me, clear in the moonlight—beautiful, open, looking up at me without expression. The arm the elf could use twisted to stab stiff fingers at the Famisher's eye—

My stomach heaved.

The Famisher squealed and shook its head hard, and the elf dropped to the ground, a limp clutter of crooked limbs. The Famisher began running in circles. It could only see out of one eye now.

From every side came ugly noises—thudding steps, sharp cries, gurgling squeals. I kept seeing things I didn't want to see.

A line of thirty or so Famishers came thundering toward the wall below me, chasing a dozen elves before them. The slower elves were grabbed, hiked in the air, and thrown away or gulped down the Famishers' huge, round maws. But suddenly all the elves spun around and dashed back among the monsters. They dodged the snaking Famisher heads and jumped onto the beasts' shoulders, trying to use their deadly cords.

They crashed against the wall below me in a churning mob, Famishers letting out these piercing screams that could have expressed either pain or triumph. I saw two elves actually running over them from one back to another, like dancers. Famishers thrashed against the walls, falling or trying to scrape the deadly riders off their backs. Right below me, Famishers tossed away mangled elves, or shook them off their huge shoulders, or were themselves choked down, lying where they fell.

Bugle-calls rang out way off to one side. Trampling and squealing, the remaining Famishers all lurched off in that direction.

The wind softened. The elves weren't laughing now, and there were fewer of them left.

Nothing moved on my side of the building anymore except two Famishers who came rooting in at the windows below me with their big round faces, like monster sunflowers. I thought of them getting inside and searching upward with those horrible heads in the dark, and maybe sniffing me out or spotting my feet or the scuffs I had left on the tree. Who knew what they could see or smell, even in the pitch dark inside Elf Home?

As quietly as I could, I edged farther out in the tree ceiling until I was in the eaves, where the edge of the roof hung over the walls. From there I could jump down and try to get away, provided I didn't break a leg when I landed. According to my memory of the map in Claudia's book, the Dalehead Arch (the closest unused one to the Tavern-on-the-Green) must be around here somewhere.

But where, which direction? I was ready to run away and try to come back another time with Kevin's knife. But I didn't dare leave the shelter of the roof.

A Famisher came snuffling around close below me. I looked down at it the way you have to look at the worst part of a horror movie even though you know you're going to hate what you see.

It had patchy, curly fur all over its humped back, like a

buffalo. But the neck was a skinny, bare buzzard-neck. The face, mercifully, I couldn't see because it had lowered its head to the ground where it was ripping away with satisfied little grunts at something hidden by the shadow of the eaves.

The only elves I could see were lying very still in the grass or else stirring just a little with movements that might have been nothing but wind tugging at their clothes. There were Famishers, too, about five of them, collapsed on the ground in large dark heaps. One of them kept rolling on its side, trying to get up and letting out a deep, raw squeal each time. Then it would flop back down, lie still a little, and try again.

Two others had dragged something out through the window and were pulling it between them, each one hanging on with its teeth and snorting aggressively through long, curled slits of nostrils like the f-holes in a violin.

The worst part was the sight and the sound of that hurt Famisher trying to get up and trying to get up, totally ignored by others of its own kind. What horrible creatures! I couldn't even think about going down there among them and trying to run away.

I hugged my branch, leaves tickling my skin. There had to be things I could do to help myself, sensible things, if I could just think of them. But you don't think much on a battlefield.

I found myself visualizing my mother longingly, seeing her as she hurried down the hall to my bedroom to wake me up from a bad dream. I thought of my dad, reading to me at bedtime from a fantasy adventure story, *The Weirdstone of Brisingamen*, a book Mom had objected to as too nightmarish. I had loved it.

But this nightmare was real. For one thing there was the

smell, now a mixture of pine scent and something incredibly sharp and disgusting—

And then the battle quit being a spectator sport.

A Famisher that had been rooting around below me lifted its head and looked up at me with huge, shining eyes.

THIRTEEN

Sobragana

WHERE WAS KEVIN, where was Rachel or Claudia, where was anybody? I was left to face this monster all by myself, without even a stick in my hand—

Except for the Farsword, of course: mighty Farfarer.

The Famisher's eyes, which were big and round and forward-facing like a cat's, blinked a slow, sleepy blink that was almost silly looking, like something a cartoon character would do to express being love-smitten. The face rose up, up on the snaky neck, as the creature reared on its hind legs. It was hugely tall. It planted its front feet on the edge of the roof with a rattling thump and looked *down* at me.

The face dropped closer, the round mouth curling open, the lips rolling inward and back to expose these incredible teeth in rows, like a shark's, all around the circular opening and deep inside the cheeks.

With a velcro rip, which made the Famisher stop and jerk its head back, I dug for the wrapped knife and pulled it out of my jacket pocket. I clamped my legs around a thick branch so I wouldn't fall and, using both hands, clawed away the cloth wrapping from the knife.

The Famisher's breath, a concentration of something like licorice to the millionth power, gusted nauseatingly over me as its face came close again. My ears rang with its squeal of pleasure. A drop of its drool splashed hot on my elbow.

Oh Mom, oh Shelly, oh Dad—but this was Kevin's world; Kevin's terms.

"Farfarer," I gasped, "you're home; be what you truly are!"

Too late—the cavern of fangs plunged toward me. I threw myself backward, imagining the killing impact of hitting the floor below. But anything was better than that disgusting creature's maw.

An underbranch of the roof tree caught me hard behind the knees. There I hung by my legs, head-down in the pitchy dark of Elf Home like a monkey in the jungle on a moonless night. I didn't drop the knife, though now it felt so heavy that I had to hold it with both hands.

I felt the close-packed leaves and branches of the roof jam hard against my left side as the Famisher's huge head punched down through the roof after me. The Famisher's neck skin, soft as a baby's, rubbed along the back of my bare hand.

I was so revolted by the touch of it that I reared up again and broke out, head and shoulders above the roof branches, gasping for breath. There, right next to me, was the Famisher's crepey, moon-pale neck, straining downward into the hole. Its blobby front hooves were set against the edge of the eaves only a few feet from me.

In my hands I no longer held a dinky little pocketknife but a sword, its blade's edge glinting in the moonlight.

As if in a dream, I hiked my arms back over my head and swung the sword down as hard as I could. The blade seemed to have a strength of its own as it slashed through the air with a rushing sound. At the last second I shut my eyes. A tingling shock shot up my arms. I clenched my teeth to keep from screaming, but screamed anyway.

So did the Famisher, or anyway it tried to: over a furious thrashing of leaves and branches echoed a horrible, liquid gurgle. The buzzard-neck reared high, headless and spouting like a garden hose.

Dark, hot blood spattered down. Frantically trying to cover my head I dropped the sword, which fell through the hole in the roof into the hall below. I never heard it land—the shavings would have muffled the sound anyway—but seconds later came the heavy crash of the Famisher's head hitting the floor, too.

The Famisher's clumsy front feet slid from the roof edge. The whole building trembled from the weight of the body falling down the outside wall.

I hugged myself to the nearest branch with all my might, gasping and gulping and still seeing that snaky neck even with my eyes strained wide. My heart beat in my chest like the footfalls of Godzilla, CRASH, CRASH, CRASH. I wanted badly to throw up.

Around me the night was silent as if, while I was having my private battle, the rest of the fight had moved somewhere else or ended, leaving me all alone on the roof without Farfarer. If I stayed where I was, I knew I would pass out and probably fall out of the stupid tree-branch ceiling and break my neck. Then it wouldn't make any difference that I had killed a monster instead of letting it kill me.

Slowly, with fumbling, sweaty hands, I worked my way through the branches down to the lowest ones, until I hung feet first, still sickeningly high above the floor. I forced my mind to picture lots of shavings heaped up right under me. I let go.

My butt and lower back hit something springy that bounced me off onto the floor with a thump: one of the piles of woven tabletops stacked around the edges of the hall had broken my fall. I got up, bruised and breathless.

There was a powerful Famisher-stink in here: heavy-duty licorice. What had Kevin been thinking of when he made them smell like that? *Candy, stupid,* I told myself. I giggled weakly and stood for a minute, making myself breathe despite the smell.

Feeling my way over to one of the windows, I looked out cautiously over the moon-washed landscape. My knees were so wobbly I had to hitch my elbows onto the deep sill of the window to stay upright. Nothing moved in my field of vision, though I saw dark lumps lying here and there in the trampled grass.

I was sweating. Without the wind of the elves' laughter, the night was unexpectedly warm. Also, I was terrified. I had just killed one Famisher, only one, and there were hundreds!

Maybe thousands! Each one was as horrible as the one I had managed by luck and desperation to destroy. I shook and cried and felt awful. Good thing it was Kevin, not me, who was the Promised Champion.

The least I could do was find the sword again. I took out the rhinestone rose, held it up and whispered, "Come on, shine a little for me, but not too much, all right?"

A bright thin beam showed me trampled shavings and long dark stains leading in a direction I had turned away from. I didn't see Farfarfer. Maybe it had turned back into a pocketknife now that it had done its work.

The rose light gleamed suddenly off almond-shaped eyes. I froze.

"Rose Traveler, I have what you seek."

By squinting hard I could vaguely make out someone sitting against the wall. I inched closer, holding the rose pin out in front of me. The little rhinestones seemed to pick up power. By their glow I saw an elf sitting there, one leg twisted under it. The whole left arm was a mangle of cloth, whatever elves have for blood, and torn muscle. Shining dark moisture smeared the wall where the elf had slid down against it.

In my mind I saw again the Famisher plucking up an elf in its jaws. I forced myself to move toward the injured elf.

My foot nudged something in the shavings—a leather bottle about the size and shape of a canteen, like the bottle Kevin had offered me a drink from on our ride to the Brangle. I imagined, at an earlier point of Prince Kavian's adventure, elves giving him one of their canteens as a gesture. Magical beings are always handing the hero special gifts to help him on his way.

When I picked the bottle up, liquid sloshed inside. I saw the elf's eyes glitter at the sound.

"I wanted that," the elf murmured. "But I had only the strength to retrieve this." The good hand opened, and in the palm I saw the pocketknife, folded shut.

I said, "I'll give you the bottle for the knife."

As soon as I said this, a ferocious thirst almost closed up my throat. But the elf smiled, and I knew we had a bargain. I knelt down, keeping an eye on the elf, and pushed the bottle across the floor.

The elf put down the knife, saying softly to me, "Call it. It will come to you."

I hesitated: a trick? But I remembered the good weight of the sword in my hands and how it had whipped through the air to save my life. It seemed natural to speak to it: "Farfarer, will you come to me?"

The knife was in my hand so quickly I barely had time to open my fingers to catch hold of it. It flared into the weight and size of its sword-form.

"No," I whispered, clutching the grip with both hands. "Be small." At once, it shrank to the cozy dimensions of a pocketknife. The plastic grip felt warm. I tucked the knife away and sealed the pocket flap carefully shut.

"I can't take out the stop," the elf said, holding up the bottle, "with only one hand."

I could hear the faint whistling undertone in the elf's shallow breath. I was afraid to go nearer. But we'd been on the same side in this battle. If I had been the one who was wounded, I knew what I would expect from a fellow fighter.

I squatted down beside the wounded elf and worked the stopper out of the bottle. The drink inside smelled of flowers. I closed the elf's slim fingers on the cool, smooth leather.

The elf drank and then inquired politely, "Did you enjoy the battle?"

Too flabbergasted to answer this amazing question, I concentrated on helping to steady the bottle against the perfect Cupid's bow of a mouth for another swallow.

"Why did you only use those string-things against Famishers?" I asked at last. "You people aren't under a vow not to use knives or swords, like Kevin—Kavian—are you?"

The elf swallowed again and panted a little. "We used cords because Famishers can't be killed by any blade until Farfarer sheds the blood of one of their great ones." An original idea of Kevin's, or something evolved by the Fayre Farre itself? Stupid, anyway.

I was dying of thirst. "What is that stuff?"

"You can drink," the elf said. "Our nectars will not harm the Rose Traveler."

I took a sip. Not the same drink as in Kevin's canteen under the kaley trees, this tasted grassy. I drank some. The elf smiled, making me feel very nervous. Had I just done something fatal?

I stood up. "I have to go," I said, "and try to find my friends." I was thinking of Rachel and Claudia, wandering around in this place that now seemed hugely more dangerous and brutal than it had before.

The elf chuckled faintly, and I recognized the tinkly mirth of the crowned one I had thought was female. "They will come to you, in time. And if you linger here—not long, I promise you—you can complete your present errand."

I didn't have any place to go, actually; not until I knew where Kevin was, or the two girls. And I had no idea where to begin looking for any of them. The drink seemed to have steadied me, making me remember the whole situation, not just my eagerness to get away.

I sat down beside the elf, trying not to groan: I had some

new bruises from crashing around at various levels of the Elf Home, and the old sore places from my first ride on a seelim and my roll in the Brangle were still sensitive.

"Complete my errand, how?" I said.

"You brought Farfarer for Kavian Prince," she said slowly, her eyelids drooping. "He will find you here."

"Somebody else could find me first," I said. "Or something."

"Oh yes," she said, and her mouth turned up in a cold elvish smile. "That is possible. The brooch you carry signals to Kavian. Farfarer sends its own call. Why do you think the hero-prince has left that weapon in your world so long? The one who carries it here on this side of the gateways draws the angry heart of the Enemy, whose name we do not speak."

Another common fantasy theme: the one who carries the magic weapon is also magically linked to the bad guy and attracts his attention the way a tall tree attracts lightning.

I must have jumped or made some move toward my pocket because the elf went on, "Be calm; the weapon only draws when it is used."

I had no intention of using Farfarer again—never had meant to. It had been strictly a matter of survival.

Still, I had a feeling Kevin was not going to be pleased when he showed up: his world, his story, and me flailing around in the middle of it with his magic sword! Maybe this elf would be my witness that I wasn't trying to horn in on Kevin's Promised Champion act or mess things up for him.

An unsettling thought struck me: Wasn't it to get away from the uproar in his own family home that Kevin had made the Fayre Farre in the first place? Yet things were no better here.

I said, "How can Kavian be coming to Elf Home? The Branglemen have got him."

"Those!" she answered scornfully. "They are animals. They know nothing. Kavian Prince will have escaped them easily. Wait here for him."

Could this elf be trying to keep me around for some reason of her own? I said, "You're telling me the truth, aren't you? You can't be on Ang—the Enemy's side. You fought the Famishers."

"Traveler," the elf said, "we fight Famishers because Famishers kill us when they can, and they do that because it is how they are made. We are made to be pretty and quick and mysterious. Do you know what happens when I die? I have no soul, having been made that way. Death is our ending, or so it is said among my people."

The calm, light voice was soothing, though the message was not. I felt tired to death. I leaned my back against the wall beside the elf, who went on, "I live among trees because they hide me and they support me, but outside our forests and meadows there is no life for any of us. When our forests burn, we die in the open sunlight. Because we were made that way."

She paused, shifting around and breathing in a stressed way that meant, I guess, that there wasn't any comfortable position for her. Her good arm came around my shoulders and drew me against her side.

I pulled away.

"Your warmth will keep me living a little longer," she sighed, "if you are willing." Ashamed, I sat still.

"We were made, as everything here was made," the elf was saying dreamily, her breath stirring my hair, "by Kavian Prince himself, whose world this is. Did you think we did not know this? Elves have secret knowledge, that is one of the things that makes us elves; and what more important secret knowledge is there than this?"

I relaxed, awed by the gift of frank speech from this royal creature. It was as if I had earned a touch of the beauty and enchantment of the Fayre Farre, having just had a good serving of its horrors.

"My blood runs out of me," the elf's voice sighed distantly, "but not my hatred; that I keep. I hate the rules we live under by command of Kavian Prince. I hate this war made to show himself off, meanwhile ensnaring and destroying us. I hate the shallow world he made for us, and I hate the way it alters at his whim, or against it, but always in relation to him.

"So tell him for me when he comes: Farfarer has been wakened, but not by him; and it has tasted evil blood, but not for him; and it has been elf-given, but not to him. Say that Elven Sobragana said it, who heard the waking and saw the blood spilled and did the giving."

"I'll tell him," I said; and as she had stopped speaking, I slept.

FOURTEEN

Farfarer

I WAS TALKING to someone whose face was unclear, complaining that Kevin had kept secret the magic sword's personal name, "Farfarer." Names are powerful in magic. Apparently he hadn't completely trusted me. It would also have been nice, I complained, if he had bothered to fill me in about elves. Did they mean what they said? Should I trust *them*? Did they mean what they said? Should I trust *them*?

"Do you have a choice?" the person said, and I

thought it was Cousin Shelly. But just as I thought this with a little surge of surprise and delight, I was dragged awake by somebody shaking me.

"Get up, Amy, wake up!"

"Talking to Shell," I mumbled, trying to dive back into my dream; but my eyes opened.

Kevin tugged at my arms, cursing under his breath.

I was freezing, and I couldn't move. Something had me pinned in place, as if I had bent double and wedged myself under a heavy table—like the time when I was real little and I got into the kneehole of Dad's desk and panicked, thinking I couldn't get out because I couldn't straighten up.

With Kevin's help, I squirmed free of what seemed to be a wooden statue of the Elf Queen. It was polished brown and smooth except where the scaly bark draped like cloth. The eyes were open and blank.

It wasn't a statue. It was her.

I began shaking all over. "I was talking with her just last night! She said if I waited, you'd come find me."

"Then she told the truth, for a wonder," he said.

I peered around, trying to square what I saw now, in this thin dawn light, with last night's chaos. The hall seethed slowly with pale mist. Everywhere tree branches and vines curled in through the windows and snaked along the walls and floor, as if through an ancient ruin overgrown by jungle. A woody brown vine had even wound itself around one leg of the petrified Elf Queen.

"They go back to the forest when they die," Kevin said, poking the queen with the toe of his boot. She rocked, her undamaged arm sticking out foolishly over the air where my shoulders had been.

I said, "Don't kick her, Kevin."

"Squeamish?" he said nastily. "Wait till you get outside and see what's left from the fighting."

"I saw plenty," I said. "Last night, if it was last night. How could trees grow this fast?"

"Elves don't breed," he said. "You know where new elves come from? The forest makes them. So the elves make new forest when they die. It all works out."

I shivered. I hadn't known Elven Sobragana well, but now I felt sorry for her. While I'd slept she had died, if not truly alone then as good as, and become this wooden statue.

"She said she hated you," I said. "I'm not sure the elves think it works out so nicely, Kevin."

"Who knows what elves think?" he said darkly. "Don't waste sympathy on them. They're modeled after the fairy-folk my mother used to talk of, and there's nothing colder-hearted than the Good People of Ireland."

"These may be different from what you meant them to be," I pointed out, thinking of the Branglemen.

"Maybe." He shrugged and turned away.

He was wearing dark blue pants and a yellow shirt with a blue vest buttoned tight over it. His Reeboks were blue, too. He was a color-coordinated hero-prince, even to the faded yellow bruise on the side of his head where the Brangleman had smacked him. The nearer we came to the final confrontation, the more fashion-conscious he seemed to get.

"Did you bring the sword?" he asked.

I nodded, but I didn't hand him the knife, not right away. I remembered what the Elf Queen had told me, and with the memory came a slow burn of anger.

"Kevin, why didn't you go get the Farsword yourself?"

"You do have it?" he said urgently.

"Yes. Answer me, Kevin."

"I told you," he said, "I had only one gate I could use, and I had to stay close to it. I was lucky to get as far into the park, as far from the arch and the Fayre Farre itself, as I needed to give you your pin back."

"I mean before that," I insisted. "There are lots of arches in the park. You must have been back and forth a whole bunch of times to use them all up—"

"There's over thirty, counting the water bridges," he said, "and every arch is different." I heard that soft, dreamy pride in his voice as he harked back to the beginnings of his fantasy, before it had gone all dark and cruel on him. "I know them all. I started the Fayre Farre with them, did I tell you that? Great names—Dalehead, Greyshot, Dipway, Glade, Winterdale, Bank Rock—I used to recite them like a spell to get me here, when I was real small."

I hung on. "You must have made a lot of trips, to use up all those gateways. But you never brought the sword back here with you. Why?"

"I already told you. I couldn't find it," he said. "Hell, I was scared to go look in the old house. I was afraid to run into my old man, if you want to know."

I froze. "Kevin," I said, "there *was* an old man, I mean a really old man, at your house, living on the ground floor—"

Had I actually come face to face with Kevin's *father*?

"My father died," Kevin said shortly. He shrugged. "Even so, I thought I might find his ghost hanging around the old place, waiting for me, too drunk and too mad to lie down."

That got to me. "My mom told me how he treated you," I said. "We're sorry if we made things harder for you, Kevin."

He grunted. "Yeah? Well, you can both stick it."

"Hey," I said, "you don't have to be so nasty. Look, I know—"

"No you don't," he interrupted. "You don't know. You think everybody's born with standard issue of a nice, happy family living in a nice, comfortable apartment with a room for each kid and plumbing that works—"

Stung, I shot back, "Hey, nobody's family is happy that way, like in some sit-com. I know that, even if you don't."

Funny, though, somehow I'd always thought of Rachel's family as happy, with her chipper little mom and her distracted-looking father who was a stockbroker during the day and went into the spare bedroom at night to play the violin. Of course there were the twins—nasty, spoiled brats, I'd seen them gang up on Rachel in a sly, subtle way that the parents didn't seem to notice—how happy were they all, really? What else went on in that house that only the family living there knew about?

"You don't know shit," Kevin snarled, kicking hard at a mound of shavings on the floor. "You never did, and you don't now." He turned and glared at me with reddened eyes. Something desperate showed there. Was this how I had looked, snarling at Mom and Dad about injustice over my rye bread? Probably. Which told me something about how Kevin must be feeling. "It's luck for some people and lickings for others, and no understanding how it's portioned out."

"It's the luck of the draw, Kevin," I said, my sympathy evaporating. Everybody got some kinds of lickings. Like— who had decided Cousin Shelly should die so suddenly and so young? "I'm sorry you had a rough childhood, but you're not the only one. You sound pretty sorry for yourself, which isn't very heroic no matter what noble title you stick on yourself."

He kicked up another clump of damp sawdust. "You talk a good game, but you're soft," he said disgustedly. "In my family you wouldn't have survived, you know that? My baby sister was tougher than you."

His kicking had uncovered this big, roundish, bloody, dirty object, like a tabletop only it wasn't. It had to be the head of the Famisher I had personally decapitated.

I wasn't tough enough for that.

"Let's get out of here," I said.

We walked out past the big entry doors that had been wrenched all crooked during the fighting. Beyond stretched a foggy field of dead: great lumpish mounds that had been Famishers and poor bundles of roots and stumps that were what was left of the elf warriors. If there was any way to tell who had won the battle, assuming anybody had, I didn't know what it was.

Kevin said, "Where were you during the fighting?"

"Hiding in the ceiling," I said.

"Huh," he said. "I never said you weren't smart. 'Course, I'm no dummy myself, remember. Even the Branglemen couldn't hold me."

"Quit boasting," I said. "You're protected. Does the mighty hero ever die in some accident on his way to his macho duel with the bad guy? Not a chance."

Kevin shook his head. "You don't understand anything at all, do you? Even after all this."

I shut up, annoyed with myself. I didn't want to fight with him, or rather I wanted to fight about real things, not get diverted into his old grudges and resentments. Only now I'd forgotten what I'd started out being angry about.

Kevin waved his hand at the silent landscape. "Let's get going. Soon there'll be Bone Men all over the place looking for the Farsword, and it's a long way from here to the castle on the Black Cliffs."

"Not for me," I said. "I've done what you wanted. I'm going home."

His mouth tightened. "Not if you're truly one of the princesses of the prophecy. It was clear, you know, anybody who heard it could tell you: the three princesses show up at the Black Cliffs for the finish."

"The other two can if they want to, but I'm through." I took the knife out of my pocket. I could hardly wait to have it out of my hands. "Here, take this, it's yours."

He backed away a step and put his hands in his pockets.

"Come on, Kevin, take it," I said.

"Why don't you come with me?" he asked. "Scared to?"

I shivered, standing there in the gray morning. "Yes," I said. It came out in a whisper.

"Hey, I'm sorry," he said, his gray eyes wide and innocent. "I guess I came down on you too hard, okay? It threw me, finding you in the middle of a battlefield. You could have been wounded."

"Or eaten by Famishers," I said, mashing down a ripple of nausea.

"Yeah," he said, "but you weren't, you did fine. I shouldn't have insulted you before—I'm sorry, honest I am. You're not some helpless weenie, whining and moaning all over the place. So look, I'd be, like, honored if you'd carry the knife for me. It would really help. Nobody would think of looking for it on a girl. You could be my squire."

Sobragana had been right: Kevin was not a prince and a Champion but a coward, a chicken-hearted sneak. I felt not just angry but disappointed and sad.

"Thanks," I said sarcastically. "I'm really underwhelmed by your graciousness, Kevin. It's about time you carried the can for yourself, okay?"

"Hey," he said, all injured but with an anxious little light in his eye, "I'm trying to be nice."

"Nice my foot," I shouted. "You set me up, you think I don't know that? Those Famishers sniffed the Farsword and came after it last night, and I was on the spot instead of you. Now you want me to go on carrying it, like some kind of lightning rod. I know how come you go questing all alone, with no crew of trusty cohorts. People get killed, protecting you! Because only the mighty hero has to get to the end of the story, never mind who else drops by the wayside. All those great warriors you said had died along the way, like poor Sebbian—they're secondary characters, perfectly disposable. Well, I'm not—got it?"

His cheeks flamed, but he didn't say anything. Fine—I had more to say myself.

"So I am not standing around to catch any more crap meant for you. The Fayre Farre is your problem, not mine. I brought your sword. Carry it yourself."

I tossed the closed knife toward him, underhand.

It spun, blurring as one of the blades somehow opened in the air, and landed point down, vibrating gently in the sod between us so that it made an eddy in the fog. And it stood as tall as my hip, no pocketknife now but a black-bladed iron sword with a grip bound in worn leather.

"What did you do?" Kevin cried in a voice of terrible pain. "How did you bring it to life? I'm the one to do that!"

He snatched at the sword hilt, stumbled, then stared in dumbstruck horror at the Swiss Army knife in his hand. He dropped it as if it were hot.

The Elf Queen's last words rang in my mind, drowning out everything else: the Farsword had been wakened, and had tasted evil blood: it had been elf-given, but not by Kevin or for Kevin or to Kevin.

By me, for me, and to me.

It was my turn to go all white in the face. Two ghostly figures in the deepening mist, it was a wonder we could still see each other. Two figures, one of them called the Promised Champion, and the other—the other the Promised Champion in fact, named so not by the Fayre Farre's author Kevin but by dying Elven Sobragana and by Farfarer itself.

I was horrified. "Kevin, I didn't mean—"

He stepped back. "Pick it up, Amy," he said hoarsely. "Come on, I want to see you pick up the weapon of the Promised Champion."

"It's yours," I said weakly. "I don't want it."

"Pick it up!" he shouted, cocking his fist at me. "Or I'll bash your silly face in!"

I wasn't going to stand there empty-handed while he threatened me. I picked up the knife.

In my hand it was at once Farfarer again, familiar and comforting. I remembered my two-handed swing at the Famisher's snaky neck. I had been half out of my mind with fear at the time, but now the memory brought a thrill of pride.

I pleaded, not with Kevin really but with the air, with the atmosphere of the Fayre Farre, as if something there—the will that made changes despite Kevin's plans, maybe—could undo this terrible mistake. "It was an accident. That Famisher was after me, it was going to chomp me! I didn't have anything else, so I—"

"The head in Elf Home?" Kevin said, blinking from some new blow that I didn't understand yet. "The Famisher head—that was Kram, one of their Great Ones. You killed him, with my sword?"

"You know those monsters personally?" I gulped. It felt weird and shivery to learn the name of the creature whose blood had stained my running shoes black.

"You've spoiled everything!" Kevin whispered, shaking his head in disbelief. "I never should have brought you into the Fayre Farre at all. I can't believe you've done this to me."

He stomped up close and screamed in my face, "I'm the Promised Champion, not you! This place is my place; it belongs to me, not to you!" He swung away again, punching the air.

"You're like all the rest of them, you damn rich kids— you think you own everything in the world! You think you can walk into my own dream place and take it from me! Damn you, damn you for your pride and all!"

The sword, which I was holding crossways as if to defend myself from Kevin's anger, suddenly seemed like a sign of shame, like something I'd stolen.

I held it out to him. "Take it, Kevin," I begged, "come on, please. We'll fix things somehow, we'll put it back the way it's supposed to be."

"Get out of my world!" he howled, his face crumpled with pain and betrayal almost to the point of tears. I would have given a lot right then to have been able to undo—well— something of what I'd done, if that could happen without leaving me dead on the field with all the dead elves and Famishers around us.

Kevin lunged at me and snatched the sword out of my hand and it became a pocketknife again. He stalked away holding it from him like a rotten fish or something, while he searched the ground intently.

I trotted after him trying to think of something to say. There wasn't anything.

He found what he was looking for: a rocky outcrop at a high point across the corpse-littered meadow from the ruins of Elf Home.

He bent and set the little red-handled knife on a flat place on the rocks. Before I knew what he was planning, he clawed up a stone the size of a street cobble and brought it down so hard on the knife that the stone rebounded out of his hands and bounced away over the springy turf.

The knife's remains lay at Kevin's feet, a little mess of steel and plastic. He kicked the bits into the air, cursing wildly.

With a deafening crash the rock that had been Kevin's anvil swung up between us. Out of the ground shot a skeleton fist the size of a baseball glove.

I sat down backward with a thump, my eyes bulging. What must have been a real giant, once, climbed out of the earth with a rattling and scraping of bone on bone and the dull clinking of dented armor. The air I gulped in to screech with stank so horribly that I gagged instead. I turned and tried to crawl away.

Huge hard fingers closed on my arm and jerked me up off the ground.

I was dimly aware of Kevin bellowing somewhere close by. I squinched my eyes shut as tightly as I could: if I saw this thing's face I was going to die right there—or rather I was afraid I wouldn't die, no matter how badly I wanted to.

The next thing I knew, I was flung upward and propelled forward into space, clamped against what felt like iron bars that burned into my side. I was smothered in a rushing current of cold, stinking air so thick and fast-flowing that I could barely breathe.

I couldn't stand it. I opened my eyes.

Below me I saw something like the double wing of an antique airplane. It was made not of wooden struts and canvas but of rags and leather stretched on a frame of bones. All the joints moved, and the whole structure creaked and shuddered as it flapped clumsily along.

Shrieking despite myself, I struggled and squirmed in

midair. Somewhere nearby Kevin cried, "Amy, don't! You'll fall!" Through the monster's rib cage I saw him pinned under its other arm.

Between the two of us reared up a towering torso that could have been a dinosaur's, made of a crazy, crooked maze of bones with no relation to a real skeleton. The head—there had to be a head!—was blocked from my sight by the bulge of the shoulder joint, which seemed to be capped with several skulls all jammed together. The two huge wings, rooted in the monster's pelvis where its legs should be, slowly rotated and scooped air below us. Everything creaked and groaned as the wind blew through the open places between the joins, where the bones were lashed together with raggedy twists of sinew.

We were the prisoners of a flying bone dragon as tall as a brownstone, with the wingspan of a 727. Something that had once been a gigantic man—maybe several men buried with their war steeds—had somehow rearranged all its jumbled bones into a winged nightmare, which now carried us away into the darkening sky.

I looked down and saw a huge hand of bone with way too many fingers locked tightly around both my ankles. The monster had tucked me under its arm with my legs doubled up under me so that I could barely move at all.

The battlefield sank away. Elf Home became a toy-sized castle and began a slow, dizzying spin to the right as the monster banked, adjusting its course northward. A wave of sickening dizzyness swallowed me into merciful dark.

FIFTEEN

The Blockhouse

I WOKE UP lying on gritty dirt, hearing a kind of slow, uneven flapping noise overhead.

Dreading what I would see—*not, please not, the skeletal horror that brought me here*—I opened my sticky, smarting eyes. I lay in a small bare room with no roof under a starlit sky. A dark flag stirred overhead on a pole, like a huge, sleepy bat stretching and curling up again. That was the source of the flapping noise.

I wasn't alone. Someone sat in a corner where two walls met, curled up with his head on his knees.

"Kevin," I whispered. He didn't move. "Kevin, is that you? Where are we?"

He said drearily, "Sky Castle on the Black Cliffs. It's supposed to be a fort against evil, but it's his place now. He's taken us prisoner, and I have nothing to fight him with."

I saw starlight twinkling in at four small windows, one in each wall. *Sky Castle?* Were we floating in the sky? Though all my stiff muscles protested, I got up and wobbled over to look out of the single little doorway.

Our cell, if you could call a roofless room that, was perched on a mountaintop. Directly ahead of me I sensed empty space. Far below spread land still hidden in night and edged with distant glints of water. From down there came hints of violent activity—a glimpse of movement by torchlight, faint shouts, and the ring of metal hitting metal.

My weary body tightened in terror, but my heart jumped with hope.

"There's a battle going on down there," I said. "It's not over yet, Kevin! Maybe the White One won't win."

"He can't lose to anyone but Kavian," Kevin answered dully, "but the Promised Champion without Farfarer is helpless."

Did the Branglemen's prophecy say that? I couldn't remember a word of it now. "Where's that . . . that thing gone, anyway? If nobody's watching us, we can run—"

Kevin lifted his head. "Run where? It's brought us to North Peak. There's all of the North Isle and the Sea of Sandigrim between us and safety, and nothing farther north but wilderness and ocean. We're prisoners here while the White One's forces fight off the Armies of the Free. He'll push them back to Sandigrim shore and wipe them out, while I sit here empty-handed."

I dragged into mental focus the park map I'd tried to memorize. The only building in the north end was a tiny blockhouse left over from the American Revolution. The rebel colonists had fortified the cliffs in case the British attacked from the Harlem flats, which lay due north across 110th Street.

The Blockhouse itself was in a wild and woodsy part of the park that was supposed to be particularly dangerous—a haunt of drug dealers, not dragons. I'd gone there on a field trip with my class.

Now Kevin and I were in the Blockhouse, in pretty much its actual Central Park form. The thick walls were made of mortared stones the size of grapefruits, and the window frames flared inward to shelter sharpshooters. Inside was nothing but a raised circular pedestal for the central flagpole. From the little doorway where I stood, a narrow flight of concrete steps led down to bare rock below.

To the north the summit fell away in steep cliffs. Southeast, around the corner from the single doorway, a gentler grade ran down to a patch of woods, crisscrossed with paved pathways linking these heights with the rest of the park.

I ducked through the doorway and tiptoed down the steps. My reaching foot touched stone without a sound, but horribly familiar pale shapes started up in front of me, gleaming white where their ragged clothes streamed in the wind. Their heavy, burned-bone stench made me dizzy.

The flying horror had sorted itself back into the forms of many skeleton men. They stood guard, hemming us in. A faint whisper of voices came from them, blurred and fretful, with a clicking, grinding undertone of bone on bone.

I could see woods beyond them, but no way in the world

was I going to try to pass those Bone Men. I scrambled back into the Blockhouse.

"There's got to be something we can do," I said.

Kevin laughed despairingly. "Dummy. You think magic means you always win?"

"Of course not, not when other people have magic, too," I said. "But we've got to keep trying. Maybe we have more going for us than you think."

"Pah!" Kevin spat. "That's how much you know about it!"

"All right," I said, "I've never made a real world. Compared to you I'm an ignorant jerk, Kevin. So enlighten me. Magic means losing, is that what you're going to tell me out of your infinitely superior wisdom?"

"It means you think you're safe in your very own place," he said in a grieving tone. "The place you slip off to when the old man staggers in pissed to the eyes and in a hitting mood, see. He can crack your bones, but your heart comes here where the strength is all in your own arm and the luck of the country favors you because it's your country. And only you know the way to it: Glen Span, Springbanks, Huddlestone, Winterdale—" He chanted the names of the arches so softly that I could barely hear him through the uproar from below and the closer, restless sounds of the watchful Bone Men.

"Only your own magic twists around and attacks you," Kevin said savagely. "And things you meant as tests become great monsters. Your soldiers die fighting for you, and your sword gets busted, and you get caught with a fool of a girl, waiting for your enemy to smash you. So in the end he wins."

"Kevin, your father's dead," I said. "You told me that."

Kevin stretched his legs out and began rubbing his right knee, as if massaging stiffness out of some old injury. "Did I?

I don't remember telling you. He got into a barroom fight with too many other guys."

A horrible, ear-splitting shriek from the battle below drowned him out. I covered my ears.

Kevin grinned sourly. "That was a Famisher's death scream. Now that Farfarer has drunk Famisher blood—thanks to you, not to me—the fighters of the Free Armies can use bladed weapons against them, too. It won't do them any good, though, not against the White One. Not without me."

The sky was turning pearly gray, and I felt the chill in the air that comes before sunrise. Kevin had terrified me all over again with his dreary certainty of disaster.

"When the sun comes up," I asked, "will the Bone Men still walk?"

"Yes," he said. "In the holdings of the White One they don't need the cover of dark. They'll keep us here till he comes and takes the seedstone off me and destroys it like he's destroyed all the other magic crystals in the Fayre Farre."

"For crying out loud, quit whining!" I yelled. "You're scaring yourself and the whole Fayre Farre to death. If you'd stop moaning and groaning, maybe you could concentrate on getting this place back under control. It's *your* world, Kevin!"

"There's nothing that's mine anymore," he said. "He always takes what he wants, even here in the Fayre Farre. *Even here.*"

He hugged his legs and rocked.

"Okay," I said furiously. "Leave it to me, then. Let a girl save your neck. You give up. I'll fight."

I ran to one of the windows and yelled out, "Farfarer, come to your master's hand!"

"Don't," Kevin said.

"Then you call the sword," I said.

He groaned. "God, girls are so stupid!"

"Listen," I said, "if the sword comes to the sound of my voice only, it'll still be my sword, not yours." Did that make sense? As much as anything in the Fayre Farre did, I guess. "Call the sword *with* me."

"It's no use." He got up slowly, like an arthritic old man. "It's too far. I'm sorry. I wish I'd done all this better."

"*Sorry!*" I squawked, thinking furiously. If Kevin was apologizing, we must really be doomed.

He turned away and pulled his fist back to punch the wall. I grabbed his arm. He shoved me away.

"Kevin!" I said, "before you do something incredibly stupid, tell me one thing. What kind of magic works with swords here? What kind of magic do the sword makers use?"

He stood still, throwing off violence and despair like a radiator throws off heat. "Fire," he said finally. "Oil, sometimes: the things a blade is forged in."

"What else?" I said. "Come on, what else?"

"Blood," he said. "What it's forged for."

Blood. Naturally.

I dug out the rhinestone pin and, without taking time to think about it, jabbed the sharp end into my palm. It hurt. I swore.

"What are you doing?" Kevin said, grabbing at me.

I dodged him and ran to the nearest window and slapped my smarting, bloody hand down on the sill. "Farfarer!" I shouted. "Come!"

Down below, the land gleamed faintly in predawn light: forested hills, distant ruins, ocean beyond. The North Isle, the White One's country, slowly showed itself.

At the fourth window, I shouted to the broken sword.

Shadowy figures sped up the bare slope of rock toward

us. The Bone Men surged together in clattering alarm—too late. Two people darted through a gap in their line and scrambled up the steps into the Blockhouse. Someone flung her arms around my neck—solid, fleshy arms—and squealed in my ear, "God, Amy, are you okay?"

"Claudia? Where did *you* come from?"

"Prince Kavian," Rachel announced, "we have something that belongs to you."

Claudia pulled off her doggie purse and upended it. The moorim hung on inside the bag, but a little heap of junk fell out into Claudia's palm. It took me a minute to recognize the fragments of the pocketknife.

Kevin groaned. "The Farsword! But *look* at it!" He said it as if he hardly remembered that he was the one who had smashed it.

Rachel sank into a crouch in the doorway, looking out. "Whoo!" she said, "that was close! We used the secret stair up the cliff to this place. My little brothers discovered it last year in the real park."

Kevin said, "What secret stair? I never put a secret stair here!"

Rachel grinned. She looked high and fierce, with her blonde hair in a wild and dirty tangle on her shoulders. "Well, somebody did."

I glanced at Kevin. "An escape route for the White One? Just in case?"

"He'd have set Bone Men to guard it," he said.

"Maybe he did," Rachel said, "but they forgot. I bet it's hard to think of everything when there's nothing in your skull but some old dirt."

"It's been so exciting," Claudia gushed. "The moorim led us to the Brangle, and the Branglefolk loaned us a boat that went through this secret water-passage underground." *A tunnel,* I thought, *another of the park transverses, probably.* "Amy, you should have been there. These incredible creatures pulled us right across this ocean, they ran along the bottom and towed us so fast. Then the sword heard you calling—"

"How did you get the pieces?" I asked, astonished. "We left them scattered all over the place."

Rachel said, "The moorims collected all the bits and brought them to the Branglemen. Your friend Scarneck said I was a Princess in gold if ever he saw one, and he handed over the pieces."

"Kevin, you hear that?" I asked.

Claudia corrected me. "We should call him Prince Kavian." She sounded smitten. Wonderful.

"But look at it," Kevin said again. "It's ruined."

Claudia asked timidly, "Isn't fantasy full of broken blades that get fixed in time for the big fight?"

I said, "Yes, but 'broken blade' means one blade, two pieces, carefully kept together. This is steel spaghetti with plastic sauce."

"There's got to be a way," Rachel said. "We've come this far. It can't stop here."

My hand tingled. I sucked at the scratch in my palm that the rhinestone pin had made.

"What happened to your hand?" Rachel said, grabbing my fingers. "Jeez, Amy, you're bleeding—Yuchh, now there's blood on my sweater!"

"Blood," I said. "You said blood, Kevin; oil or blood is magic for a sword in the Fayre Farre."

He squinted suspiciously at me in the dim light. "So what if I did?"

"Blood to make the blade; blood to mend the blade," I said. "How do we do it?"

"Ask your girl friends," he said. "Everybody but me seems to know all the answers."

Claudia looked gooily sympathetic, but Rachel rolled her eyes grandly at me, signaling: this guy is a pill. I nodded vigorously, and she hid a laugh.

The flag went *flop, flop,* overhead, a little faster in the morning breeze. The sounds of battle below swelled again, nearer—screams and shouts blended into an on-again, off-again roar. Where was Anglower, anyway—down there, fighting? How long did we have until he stormed in here to squash Kevin like a bug, and us with him?

I said, "Let's try what boys would do in a secret clubhouse; what comic-book heroes would do."

"Oh," Rachel said. "That's easy. I've read the twins' comic collection. Give me the pin." I handed her the rhinestone rose. She stepped up onto the flag pedestal. "Give me your hand, Prince Kavian," she said grandly.

Kevin hesitated, then poked his hand out like a dead fish. Rachel grabbed it and jabbed the pin into his palm. He yelled. Still gripping his hand, Rachel gave me back the pin, which I sealed into my jacket pocket again.

"Now yours," she said, grabbing my hurt hand, which made me wince.

"Does this have to be so melodramatic?" I said. I didn't know what Rachel had in mind, exactly, and I was nervous.

She said, "If the sword is to go back to the prince, here, we need his blood, too. Your blood to give it up; his blood to take it."

Now I caught the drift of what she was thinking, and I jumped back with a gasp. I realized, too late, that I shouldn't even have let her stick Kevin with the pin, which still must have my blood on it.

Kevin chuckled nastily. "What are you worried about,

Amy? Look, there's war and pain here but not AIDS, all right? Whatever people do in the real world, here their blood is clean."

We all must have looked pretty scared and skeptical.

"It's the seedstones," he said. "They purify. You and I are both carrying them. Our blood's okay."

"Say that with the moorim on your head," I said.

He did, and the moorim leaned down and licked the bridge of his nose. Rachel looked at me. I nodded: the moorim's kiss was good enough for me.

At Rachel's nod, Claudia carefully dumped the remains of the knife into my sticky palm. Rachel turned Kevin's hand over and squeezed our two hands together on the bits. Claudia began humming a flat, dull tune through her nose; something she'd picked up from the moorim, from the sound of it.

Our hands, joined on the weapon, quickly heated up way past plain old 98.6. Kevin breathed hard and stood leaning back as far as he could get, his lips twisted in a grimace. I gritted my teeth: I could do as well as he did. Our knuckles began to glow. I shut my eyes.

But I couldn't stop feeling the heat intensify and creep up my wrist. I fought down panic and concentrated on the touch of sunlight on my face.

Deep in the furnace that had been my hand and Kevin's hand, something moved.

"Do you give Farfarer to the Prince?" Rachel was yelling in my ear. I hadn't realized, I was groaning so loudly through my clenched teeth. "Amy, do you hear me? Do you give Farfarer—"

"Take it, Kevin, for crying out loud!" I bawled.

Rachel let go, and Kevin and I each staggered backward.

But in his hand he held a gleaming sword, the sharp edge of the dark blade still glowing red with heat.

"Prince Kavian!" I gasped, hugging my own hand to my chest. I didn't dare look down to see if my fingers were crisped. "Farfarer is yours!"

"Farfarer is yours!" Rachel announced, hopping off the pedestal with a triumphant whoop.

Kevin blinked uncertainly at the sword as if he didn't really believe in it. Then he jumped up onto the pedestal and waved Farfarer over his head. The blade caught the rays of the risen sun with a golden flash. He shouted out over the battlefield below, "White One, I'm ready for you! Come fight me for the Fayre Farre!"

"Come to you?" sang a strong, beautiful voice from somewhere close above us. "I am already here."

We all looked up. Now we could see the design on the sunlit flag: a spiky, armored shape in a horned helmet with crimson pupils gleaming out of black eye slits. The image swelled and shook itself free of the flag, and the White Warrior stepped down inside the stone walls of the Blockhouse with us.

SIXTEEN

The Power of the Rose

HE SWUNG his gauntlets wide apart, spreading space with the backs of his huge, armored hands. Clouds of pulverized mortar puffed up from the Blockhouse walls as they rocked back and began snapping outward in a flurry of angles, duplicating themselves faster than my eyes could follow. New walls grew from the old ones, crashing into place all down the backslope of the cliffs, and a windstorm of displaced air threw me off my feet.

I could feel the ground under me swell and stretch, making room for the walls as they expanded like the interlocking pieces of a gigantic, moving puzzle. In one long roll of tremendous thunder—under the clear sky and pale white sun— a castlelike labyrinth appeared, spreading out and downward from the summit over where the woods had been. Acres of rusty tile roofs on top of ashy gray walls made of boulders the size of Volkswagens blanketed what had become a mile or more of black stone slope.

We were stuck on a sort of wide terrace, the highest point of the whole huge structure, overlooking the cliffs—black crags and empty air—and the battle below.

It was sickening, this blotting out of our dinky little Blockhouse on its poky knob of rock by this humongously swollen version of the same basic design—a simple rock-walled room.

The central pedestal was gone. In its place stood a platform of bones, yellow and white and gray. At the center stood this massive chair, made of bones twisted like wickerwork. The armored newcomer settled himself into this throne of decay. Even sitting down, he towered above us.

I hugged the gritty earth. My fear drove every other feeling out of me. There was barely room for one thin breath of air after another.

Lazing there on his sharp-toothed throne, he was a cartoon nightmare turned real: a human-shaped figure big as a bull, covered entirely in scarred white armor that jutted everywhere into jagged points and edges. His helmet crested, between wide-set horns, in a silver plume. His gloves had steel spines set between the knuckles.

"Darth Vader's paler brother," Rachel whispered to me, with a ghastly, hollow giggle.

Claudia, crouching beside us clutching her doggie purse, whimpered faintly.

Rachel said, "It's dumb, groveling around like this." She climbed shakily to her feet. I managed to do the same, though I couldn't think why I bothered. We were done for, unless our hero, the famed Promised Champion of the Fayre Farre, came through in the crunch.

He stood a little way from us, sword in hand. His mouth hung open in ridiculous dismay. Kevin Malone, Corner Kid and hero-prince, appeared to be rooted to the ground, a terrified boy with a weapon he was scared to try to use.

"Listen," Rachel said to the world at large, "it's so quiet. Is the battle over now down there?"

"Go look," answered the beautiful, ringing voice of the White Warrior. I dared to hope: maybe he was really a good guy under there, Kevin's best buddy pretending to be bad to test him, some wise and handsome god with rewards to hand out when the test was passed. No villain could speak in a voice like that.

He pointed toward the cliff, a sudden movement that rattled the spikes on his gloves and made me flinch. In my mind's eye, I saw him wipe his mask up over his head like a welder's shield and pick his yellow fangs with the needles projecting from his gloves. Now it registered, in a numb sort of way, that many of the skulls and bones that made up his throne were small, delicate shapes—maybe moorim-bones. Maybe the bones of children.

My stomach lurched, and I thought I might have to sit down again.

Rachel, who had wobbled her way over to the edge of the cliff, called me. "Amy, you should come see this."

The seated monster made no objection. I went, my spine prickling.

Below the cliffs, slanted fields and forests were thick with figures: slender elves, gnarly little Branglefolk, Famishers staring up with their round faces like clusters of ugly flowers, men in dark leathery-looking armor on foot or mounted on see-lims. The different groups had moved apart from each other, and seemed to be all waiting for—what?

"Where are the Bone Men?" I said.

"The Bone Men," replied Anglower in that glorious voice, "those mighty warriors of the bloody past, are wherever I want them to be and whatever I want them to be."

He reached down and casually plucked a long, yellow bone from the platform under his throne. He flipped it in the air. Soaring, it shook itself out into a gangling human frame which landed bent-kneed, like a ski-jumper. The skeleton straightened and began stalking toward us with long strides. Its feet made dry, scraping noises on the rock.

Rachel and I grabbed each other and huddled together at the cliff's edge. I felt empty space at my back and saw myself flying, falling, gone.

The Bone Man halted. It rocked gratingly on its heel bones and wrapped its long arms around its rib cage. It had no lower jaw, which for some reason struck me as particularly horrible.

The White One laughed, a bright, shocking sound, like ice water poured suddenly into your ears. He turned away from Rachel, Claudia, and me. His business was with Kevin, who still stood gaping like a moron.

Anglower rose from his chair and yanked another bone from the dais: a long, heavy, curved bone with a thick end. He flung it high over our heads, like an ivory lance. In flight, the bone exploded. Fragments rained on the armies below like chalky darts.

Everyone scattered, shouting, screaming. Some fell. Then they drifted together again and stood as before, gazing up toward us.

"No fair, attacking Kevin's men," Rachel yelled, outraged. Where did she get all this fearless energy? She scared me to death, challenging the monster like this. "You're supposed to fight a duel, *mano a mano!*"

The White One didn't even look at us. The armies below made no sound. They knew that it was all up to the Promised Champion and the White Warrior.

"Shush, Rachel," I hissed. "There's nothing we can do. It's Kevin's fight, fair or not."

"So why doesn't he *fight?*" Rachel said in a furious, tearful voice.

Kevin's cheeks flamed as if he'd been slapped. But he didn't raise the sword or say a word.

"If only I had a rock," Rachel said, staring desperately around, "a chunk of wood, a brick—"

"A weapon," I said. I thought of Kevin in the laundry room of the D-home, backed against a wall, unarmed except for—my brain seemed to catch fire. " 'Using a weapon they already own!' *The rose pin!*"

I jumped up, fumbling in my pocket, yelling about magic crystals—the rhinestones: wouldn't they work against the White One?

I had forgotten the Bone Man.

He tackled me, crashing into my knees with an excruciating impact. Rachel flung herself at him, trying madly to drag away the spindly hand that was knotted into my hair. I heard Claudia shrieking.

With the strength of total panic, I ripped my arm free and clapped the rhinestone pin against the side of the Bone Man's skull.

The whole figure fell apart, leaving me flat on my back in a scatter of bones. But the bones reared up into a new shape faster than my eyes could follow. More bones came clicking and rolling over the rock from the White One's dais and wove themselves together with the speed of snakes striking. They surrounded Rachel and me with a cage of bent and woven bone while Claudia crouched, blubbering, outside.

The triumphant laughter of the White Warrior washed over us. Then, with a clacking sound, the lid banged down. Two of us were penned up in a cage of bones, and the third one was a quaking mound of terror outside of it. I could see that Claudia wasn't going to be any help.

At last Kevin spoke: "Let them go!" he screamed. "You can't touch them, you don't lay your hand on them—not in my country!"

Through our cage of bones we saw him charge, swinging Farfarer two-handed in a sweeping, side-to-side stroke. The White Warrior smashed down at him with the long bone he held. Kevin dodged the blow, but the knuckle-end hit rock and the whole summit shivered. I heard crackings and rumblings deep in the mountain below us.

"He'll smash the place apart!" Rachel cried, for the first time sounding panicky, as if the reality of our situation had just dawned on her. "He'll wreck the whole Fayre Farre!"

The rhinestone rose lay in my palm, its stones crushed and blackened. I scraped it against the bone cage, but it had no effect now. I dropped the ruined brooch into my side pocket again and sealed the flap.

Farfarer made deep, whipping sounds through the air. The White One's bone club slammed the blade aside again and again, until Kevin pulled back, panting. Instead of attacking him, the White One reached down, grabbed up a skull with his free hand and lobbed it out over the battlefield below.

Spinning, the skull dropped from view. We heard a distant, thunderous impact and howls of terror.

Kevin cursed wildly and closed in again, sweat flying from his hair. *Berserk,* I thought. *That's how you fight when you're berserk; that's what it means.*

Under the cliffs the Free Armies' soldiers were singing a ragged, rousing tune.

"He's winning; I think Kevin's winning," I chanted under my breath.

Rachel panted, "That won't help *us* Amy—this cage is getting smaller!"

I realized with horror that I had been vaguely aware for a couple of minutes of more and more pressure where my skin touched the bonework. I braced my back against Rachel's and my hands and feet against the dry, rough bones.

"Claudia! Help!" I screamed. "We've got to get out of here!"

But Claudia lay scrunched up on the rock, covering her head with her purse.

Anglower hacked at Kevin's legs with his club. Kevin parried with a slice that cut the bone club to half its length. Kevin lunged, but the White One dodged, pivoted, and kicked the edge of the bone dais under the throne.

A shower of bones sprayed out over Kevin, who ducked and covered his head. Blood spread from a dozen cuts made by flying fragments right through his clothes. *It wasn't fair!*

"I can't breathe," Rachel gasped, her spine and shoulders heaving and shoving against mine.

Claustrophobia choked me. My stiffened arms were now slowly but surely buckling at the elbow, and the top of the bone cage was touching my hair.

Backing toward us, Kevin clawed his handkerchief out of his back pocket. He blotted a cut on his forehead with it, then stopped, swore, and bent to tear madly at the corner of the cloth with his teeth: Kevin's seedstone, the rhinestone from my pin, was in there.

He ran at the White Warrior, who waited for him empty-handed now, flexing the spines on his gauntlets. I imagined Kevin impaled on those spikes, lifted from the ground with the force of the blow.

But Kevin ducked a swing of one armored fist and leaped up against the White One's massive chest like a basketball player doing a mighty slam-dunk. I saw him slap his hand to one eyehole of the gleaming helmet, and drop the tiny seed-stone inside. Spinning away, he landed in a crouch and flung his arm up over his eyes as a flare of blinding white light blossomed around the White One's horned head.

When I could see again, I saw a wonder: from the top of the helmet down, the white armor silently peeled away and fell off like sections of shell from a hard-boiled egg.

Inside was a man, just a man: a little taller than Kevin, lankier, a lot older. He wore faded jeans with ironed-in creases, work boots, and a T-shirt under a tan windbreaker. His jaw was blue with whisker-shadow, and deep lines were cut into his cheeks, bracketing his mouth. He stared at Kevin with a puzzled frown.

Oh, I thought, dizzy with relief: *it's just a man. Just a person, somebody we can talk to.*

As I thought this, Kevin threw himself into battle again with a terrible, tearful wail. But he fought in slow motion now, sobbing as he moved, grunting with each swing of the sword. The stranger who had been the White One scowled and smacked the blade away each time with his bare hands, retreating unhurriedly toward the castle wall behind him. In-credibly, no blood flew, only tears that Kevin dashed from his own eyes with his free hand.

"We fixed the sword," I gasped, shoving frantically against the inexorable tightening of the cage walls as they shrank in on us. "Why can't Kevin touch him?"

Rachel whispered, "Don't you see? That's his father."

I said, "His father's dead."

"It's not his real father," Rachel said hoarsely. "Worse. A shadow of his father, the Branglemen say. A memory. You can't hurt a ghost!"

Through the distortion of my tears, I could see the muscles of Kevin's back and shoulders stand out as he dragged the sword through the air again, like pulling it through deep water. I was so sorry for him. He must have brought a version of the real-world monster, his father, to the Fayre Farre to be the bad guy, the one who loses in the end.

But his father was too strong. Kevin, still only a boy, was no match for him.

Suddenly I felt something small moving on me and I heard an unlikely sound: the sound of velcro tearing. My pocket flap was opened, and delicate paws reached in and drew something out.

"Oh, my God, she's gone!" Claudia screamed, staring down into her purse. "Oh, my God, Amy, Moorie's in there with YOU!"

In, but trying to get out again: hard little feet dug for purchase at my hip. I looked down but couldn't see; my own arm was in the way, and I had nowhere to move it.

Claudia screamed, "She's coming back out! She's squeezing through, she's getting out! Oh, my God," she keened, "she's hurt, she got mashed, she's bleeding!"

I had nothing to spare for the moorim. Before my eyes, the enemy stepped suddenly forward, wrenched the sword out of Kevin's hands and hurled it aside. It bounced off the edge of the cliff and out into space. Kevin's father reached out and contemptuously shoved him in the chest. Kevin stumbled backward and fell. He got to one knee and knelt there, exhausted, both hands braced on the rock, like a sprinter with no strength left to race.

Claudia said softly, "Moorie gave me your pin, Amy. Now there's moorim blood on it."

Rachel twisted in the cage, grinding my backbone in half. "It's all we have—even burned out, it's still the weapon we already own!"

My numb mind wouldn't work. Staring straight ahead through the tightening bone bars, I saw the ghost-double of Kevin's father spit on the ground and pull the leather belt he wore out of the belt loops of his clean, pressed blue jeans.

I moaned, "The prophecy lied, then! What good is a beat-up old pin?"

"It's like something from a grave," Claudia murmured, somewhere close to my left ear—I couldn't turn my head to look at her. "It's all twisted and burned-looking, like something buried in the ground for a thousand years."

Years—the word bounced around inside my skull. *Years. Solve the great riddle of using the years . . . Using a weapon they already own—*

Cousin Shelly had given me the rose brooch, a pin in the shape of a climbing rose vine, gift from a person who loved plants and gardens and used them as a kind of antidote to all the horrible stories of ruined families that came at her every day in her work. A symbol of living growth against an avalanche of suffocating misery.

The man lashed his belt down across Kevin's hunched shoulders with a horrible cracking sound.

I didn't know the answer to the riddle, but I knew what to do.

"Claudia," I said. "Plant the rose pin. There are cracks in this rock. Stick Shelly's pin down one of them, quick!"

I couldn't see her, the way my head and shoulders were jammed tight in the bone cage, but I heard her crying. "Moorie got squeezed to death by the bones. She's dead, poor little thing. We hardly even got to know each other."

"The pin," I said choking. "Plant it or the moorim died for nothing, and we'll all die, too."

In front of me, Kevin moved slowly backward on all fours. The man followed, snapping the belt between his fists. He looked like murder, a million times scarier than that puffed-up cartoon, the White One. I hated him with a scalding hate, for Kevin and for all of us.

"There," Claudia said softly, moving back into my field of vision and brushing her palms together.

Instantly the earth bucked and the bone cage flew apart with a tearing shriek, spilling Rachel and me out like Monopoly dice shot from a box. Something erupting from the rock under us had exploded our prison. A giant? Who cared? All I wanted was to get real air into my lungs, and to straighten my aching arms and legs.

The whole peak seemed to be shivering and crumbling with the some tremendous uprush from below. Maybe the North Isle was volcanic? Were we about to be spewed out over the Fayre Farre in a shower of molten lava?

My teeth chattered madly and my skin was iced in sweat: panic mode in the old body. I hugged the shaking ground.

Kevin's father stood brace-legged on the shivering cliff. Kevin, crouching at the edge, rocked not only with the movement of the mountain but with the effort to get enough momentum of his own to stand upright. His shirt was torn, a red stripe was burned across one shoulder, and tears slicked his cheeks. I could see his lips and throat spasming with sobs, and I knew he would throw himself off the cliff rather than take that strap across his back again.

With a crackling hiss like millions of small, wet explosions at once, whatever had demolished the bone cage whipped up and caught the man's ankle, yanking him off balance. Something flung itself up his thin body, a swarm of snakes—no—a net of stems and branches, growing at fantastic speed and putting out leaves, flowers.

A humongous plant squirmed and sprouted out of the split stone peak, unfurling a staggering mass of thorny stems, leaves, and blossoms. Roses as big as babies' heads burst wildly into bloom higher than I could have reached.

In seconds Kevin's father was overwhelmed and pulled down in a bank of climbing roses, his shape lost in the quivering, vinelike stems. The blur of growth spread like spilled paint over the remains of the dais and the throne and poured out over the edge of the cliff in a green cascade starred with flowers.

The ground stilled; the thunder died away. We kids were left on a mountaintop covered—except for a few bare ridges of stone—with roses.

Claudia grabbed my arm. "Look—Kevin's gone crazy!"

Kevin was dancing at the cliff's edge, kicking his legs up into the air and shouting breathless shouts of victory. Cautiously, we made our way to him, walking—limping—on the rocky ridge paths.

"He's caught!" Kevin yelled. His eyes glittered wildly. "He can't do anything!"

The phantom of Kevin's father lay tangled in roses just at the head of the great fall of them over the lip of the cliff. Flowers opened all around him as we watched. He strained to free his hands, blinking up at us with bloodshot, angry eyes.

"Kevin, get me out of this," he said in a reedy voice, tearing one hand free and raising it to shield his eyes from the sunlight. "What are you waiting for? Do as I say. I am not too drunk to thrash you, boy."

Instead of answering, Kevin stooped and tore rose vines up with both hands. With all his strength he lashed them down on his trapped enemy, as if flailing a whip, a cat of twenty thorny tails.

The man covered his eyes with his arm, crying out in a language I didn't know. Sobbing, Kevin hauled the vines back with bleeding fingers to strike again.

The man groaned and rolled over, burrowing down into the bed of blooms and thorns. His free hand clawed into the tangle of rich growth alongside him, and as he turned, he lifted it and dragged it over his head and body like a blanket. The bank of roses rolled him under, covering him deep and hiding him from the sun and from our stupefied eyes.

"What did he say?" Rachel whispered. "I couldn't understand him."

Panting, Kevin answered, "He said, 'Oh father, do not strike me again, for I fear that I shall die.' He said it in Gaelic. But I'm not his father. Why did he say that to me?"

"Not to you," Claudia said. "To his own father." She blotted her eyes on her sleeve. "Where do you think he learned to be such a monster?"

From the battlefield below, voices rang. Famishers and Bone Men don't sing. We had won.

Kevin dropped the whip of roses, which had ripped his shirt and raked deep scratches into his arms and hands. His face was streaked with sweat and blood and his dark hair was plastered to his cheeks. He answered bitterly, "Well, he'd better be dead now. Nobody will cry for him, either. Nobody. He should have died a long time ago, before he ever had children of his own."

The nearest roses turned and swayed to catch the drops of his blood and his tears on their petals of velvet red.

SEVENTEEN

Prince's Choice

"LONG LIVE THE PRINCE!" someone shouted. "Hail to our Champion!"

We rode slowly across the battlefield, trailed by a self-appointed honor guard. My whole body ached from almost being squashed in the bone cage, and Rachel must have felt the same. One of the elves had handed a canteen to Rachel, and whatever was in it—slightly warm and sharp like cranberry juice—had perked us all up. Still, slowly was all we could manage.

A man Kevin had identified as Sebbian's brother had met us at the foot of the Secret Stair with some tired and mud-splashed seelims, one of them my blue-green one, which I now rode. From its back I got to wave at an admiring throng who were all waving at me. The Branglemen clicked their throwing clubs together in a rattling racket as we rode by. It was a thrill.

Our victory was total. The Bone Men on the battlefield had fallen under the rivers of roses that seemed to hunt them out among the fighters. The Famishers had been killed or driven away bleeding and screaming.

Corpses lay all over the place. That part was not thrilling. War kills. If you want to know more, go look at the photographs Mathew Brady took after the Union and Confederate armies had pounded each other to bits at Gettysburg.

On the trampled meadows and hummocky hills all dark with blood and veined with roses, they called our names and shouted blessings and thanks. Prince Kavian, they called him; and they called us princesses, which made Rachel toss her hair and say she hadn't planned on becoming such close family so fast. We did a lot of kidding around. We were silly with relief. It was easy to get high on all the cheering.

The sun dropped lower. I began to feel nostalgic for my own bedroom. Probably everybody around us was dreaming about home. It made another part of the bond that linked all of us victorious survivors.

Behind Kevin and me, Scarneck walked between Claudia's seelim and Rachel's. Sebbian's brother, a large man with his left arm in a sling, wearing homemade armor of battered iron, rode beside a gangly kid I didn't know. Kevin had greeted this boy, Danu, like a long-lost brother. Three slender elves kept up easily on foot. I wondered if there was *ever* such a thing as a fat elf.

No one spoke Anglower's name. I saw no trace of him, only the downspill of roses from the mountaintop.

"He wasn't what you expected, was he?" Kevin asked suddenly, as if he'd read my mind. "The White One."

"No," I said. "But he was something, Kevin."

"He was," Kevin said grimly. "The mighty warrior in shining armor with a magic voice. That's how he always painted himself when he talked about the Old Country. But my mother said Pa was never even in Ireland. He was born here. It was his own father's stories he was adapting to tell, as if he'd done all those heroic deeds that probably Granda hadn't done, either. What Pa did, himself, was get drunk and come home and kick his family around when the mood took him, which was often."

"That's terrible, Kevin," I said.

"Well, it's over." He reined his seelim toward the east. "This way. The elves are making a victory feast tonight."

We rode east below the highlands surrounding North Peak, and then around a wide, shallow lake with boggy margins that made the seelims honk and pick up their feet high in a disgusted manner. We came out on a grassy plateau facing the bottom of the mountain across a shallow green valley.

The valley had once been a lake with floating gardens on it, Kevin said, which the original Elf Home on the ridge had overlooked. That was before Anglower had taken over North Isle and driven the elves south.

A lake—ha, I thought: *the Lasker Rink, at the very northeast-most corner of Central Park. And the old Elf Home had stood where the boathouse had once been, the one that Claudia's book said had burned down.*

Elves had made a new home in the hours since the battle, wedging together the treelike statues of their dead warriors. You could see hands and arms and faces and feet jammed more or less flush to make the walls.

On the green bank around the hall, men and Branglefolk tended the roasting carcasses of animals and birds. I didn't look too closely. I'd seen enough dead things for a lifetime.

Inside, the hall was packed. Elves on the balcony blew curved horns in tremendous fanfares, and the mob of battle-stained fighters roared out our names as we entered.

There was an earthen dais at the back, and the crowd parted to make a rough pathway to it. One by one we were handed up to sit on enormous chairs so encrusted with gems and gold that they would have been impossible to actually sit in, if not for the heaps of rather moth-eaten and dusty cushions.

"Where did this stuff come from?" I whispered.

Claudia tucked her legs under her on the seat—her feet didn't reach the ground anyway—and said, "Troll treasure, Amy. You wouldn't believe what we saw on the way here with the sword pieces."

"It was all part of Kevin's epic," Rachel put in from her own throne. Her face was flushed with excitement and her hair was a mess. She looked great.

I suddenly felt terrible. My best friend had been off sharing private adventures with Claudia while I was struggling along with old Kevin for company. Maybe I had missed all the best parts. Maybe Rachel really wasn't my friend any-more.

Kevin stood up to acknowledge the cheers of the crowd. Sore and tired from the fight, he didn't raise his arms in a victory salute. But he stood straight and held his head up. And you know what? He looked great, too.

I cheered with everybody else. What else could I do?

There was food, music, uproar, and more food for what seemed like hours. I ate myself to sleep, right where I was. Since I was a princess, I guess nobody minded.

Then Kevin was shaking my shoulder to wake me, and the hall was quiet, dim, and stale smelling. For one horrible second I thought I was back at Tavern-on-the-Green, with Elven Sobragana dead and Kram's huge head seeping blood into the scattered chips on the floor. But Rachel and Claudia stood in front of the throne-mound.

"Your friends want to leave," Kevin said. "Are you going with them?"

I got up carefully. I was stiff and sore all over. Aspirin would have been nice, but I didn't bother asking. They are not big on analgesics in heroic fantasy; they just push along, bleeding and gritting their teeth.

"Sure," I said. "What about you, Kevin?" Funny. I wanted him to come, too, as if he had a home to come to.

"I've used all the gates," he said. His voice had no expres-sion.

"Hey," I said, "you've got three princesses here, remem-ber? We can get you through."

Rachel said, "I already told him that. He won't listen."

Claudia looked uneasy. "Maybe it's better if he stays here."

Rachel said, "Come on. This isn't a real place!"

"It is to me," Kevin said.

Outside somebody was singing, flat and hoarsely, and I heard other voices arguing and laughing and somebody hammering metal. It all sounded pretty real to me, too.

Claudia said, "I've gotta go, really. Zia Cynzia is going to KILL me as it is."

Rachel said, "They're saddling seelims for us now, Amy. Meet you outside in ten minutes, okay?"

They left. Kevin and I were alone in the hall.

"How do we get home from here, anyway?" I asked. The north end of the park didn't have many arches, according to what I remembered of the map.

Kevin moodily kicked the base of one of the thrones. "You can go back through the Glen Span, it's a straight shot west."

He was serious about staying; which probably meant I would never see him again. I realized suddenly that I minded. I minded a lot. I think I had some crazy idea of him coming back and living with my family until he could work something else out. Maybe I thought we could make up for the childhood he'd never really had.

I said, "How do you know you *can* stay? What if the Fayre Farre spits you out somehow, now that you've finished your quest? End of story, poof!"

"That's not much of a risk compared to some of the chances I've taken around here. You don't even know." His brooding stare told me I didn't want to, either.

An idea went off in my head like lightning.

"Hey," I said, "listen, I'd *like* to know. I bet everybody would. If you come home and write it, Kevin, my dad might be able to sell it for you, for big bucks in Hollywood, and I mean *big*."

Kevin smiled a down-turned, sardonic smile. "Oh, sure.

You think I don't know the Fayre Farre is a mishmash of stolen ideas?"

"So what?" I said. "Have you read what's out there lately? It's all like that. But your Fayre Farre really lives; it's a terrific creation."

He waved at the empty, littered hall. "The life of it is here, not in my head. I couldn't put it on paper, I'm no author. But I might be a pretty good prince."

"Come on, what do you know about running a world? I mean really *running* it, as a—a politician, not a hero on a quest."

"Oh, right," he bristled, "what's the dirty-faced kid from down the block doing wearing a crown?"

That hurt. "That's not what I mean, and you know it!"

"Well, damn it," he yelled back, "I'm responsible, you understand me?" He began to pace up and down in front of the dais, scowling at the earthen floor. "People fought and died to put me on the throne of the Fayre Farre. I can't just ride off into the sunset. I have to stick around and make sure things turn out all right."

I made myself answer reasonably, like a grown-up. "Things don't turn out. They go on and on and change all along. So you're talking about being here for good. But this is a dream, Kevin. Real people can't live in dreams. You'll go crazy here."

Silence. Then he said, "They need somebody in charge, and they're counting on me to make things hang together now."

"I don't get it," I said. "What's falling apart?"

"Everything!" He waved his hands in the air, then jammed them into his pockets. "There's already been a fight between two Branglemen and some elves over something I can't make out. Danu says the human men want to know if the elves' hall being rebuilt here means that the elves are staking a claim to the whole North Isle. Now that Elven Sobragana's gone, there's some very expansionist factions speaking up among the elves. Old grudges are surfacing all over the place."

"What makes you think you can fix that?" I said. "Or that you should? Kevin, let them work things out themselves here."

"It's not that simple," he insisted, shaking his head. "Old grudges are terrible things. They can keep people at each other's throats for generations. I can't let it be like that here. They'll listen to me. I beat the White Warrior."

"Yes, you did." I shuddered. "But, Kevin, what if he comes back?"

Kevin's shoulders hunched involuntarily. "Comes *back?*"

"He was beaten before," I said, "according to all that history you told me. But he came back."

"He did," Kevin said, biting his lip. Then he nodded once, short and sharp. "That's the clincher. I can't leave the Fayre Farre unprotected, you see? It has to be as strong as I can make it, in case he *does* come back."

I licked my dry lips and said what had to be said. "But what if it's you that draws him, Kevin?"

"All the more reason," he said harshly. "If I draw him to me, well, best do it here in my country, where I'm a prince and a hero, not in your world where I'm just a tough kid. Well, wouldn't you do the same, in my place?"

In a way this was the most flattering thing he could have said to me. It was also the end of the argument, I knew that. So I stepped up close and kissed his cheek quickly before he could pull away. "Good luck, Kevin."

I meant it, too. Maybe in his place I wouldn't have done

the same, but so what? The White One was never my father; and the Fayre Farre was not my creation, it was his.

So I turned and walked out of the hall ready to go home, but without Kevin Malone. The Promised Champion was already home.

EIGHTEEN

Troll and Silver

HALF THE COMBINED Free Armies trailed along southward with us that morning on foot or on see-lims, talking and singing like the biggest, most heavily armed picnic you ever saw.

We reached a wide river, Kevin's version of a little stream called the Gill in Central Park. Riding west along its course, I heard a distant booming that warned me to expect rip-roaring falls instead of the neat little cascades of the Gill.

By this time it was midmorning, with the cool light filtering spookily through huge trees onto the leafy forest floor around us. It felt sort of rude to come bustling through there with all the noises that a huge mob of people on the move makes. I wished I could have had time to enjoy it alone and in peace.

The elves began to sing, high, interweaving sounds that echoed away among the upper branches like the calls of birds with bells in their throats. Walking alongside my seelim, Scarneck translated: it was about how these trees were the ancestors, ancient and patient, of the southern elves, and that these ancestors rejoiced at their descendants' return.

"Not true," Scarneck commented angrily, showing his yellow canines. "All was Brangle here, before the Cold People ever came."

"Where did the elves—the Cold People come from?" I said.

"Over the sea," he said, jabbing his wooden lance in a vaguely northern direction. "And they should go back there."

Kevin was right, there was trouble ahead.

I watched Kevin riding alongside Danu, who kept talking and laughing, amusing his hero-friend whom he obviously worshiped. At least Kevin had a friend here, a kid his own age. He and Danu could have been brothers, I thought.

As my seelim picked its way prissily among the trees, a whole new story unrolled in my head: Danu could turn out to be a long-lost sibling, a rival for the crown, and end up joining with the ambitious duke in the south. Maybe here in the Fayre Farre it was the name "Danu," not "Dan," that was marked somewhere on the Farsword, maybe—

Claudia urged her seelim up beside me and put something into my hand. "Singer gave me this to bring to you. He stayed home in the Brangle, but he said to tell you that he won't forget 'The Muffin Man.' "

It was a polished silver coin with some kind of flying figure embossed on it—like the horrible flying bone dragon-man who had carried Kevin and me over the Sea of Sandigrim to the North Isle. I almost threw the thing away into the forest.

But the coin was from Singer, a friend. I kept my hand in my pocket, the coin gripped in my fist. Did I want to carry anything home with me from Kevin's country? Would that somehow give him a hold on me, something to use any time he felt like bringing me here again?

Or was it something I could use to come here again on my own? I was feeling homesick for this place already. Maybe there's a forest like Kevin's forest of North Isle in the dream-world of every city child who ever played in a park.

The waterfall was wide and furious as expected. We rode through air tingling with spray along a narrow trail inside a steep gorge. Up ahead at the point where the walls of the ravine seemed to meet, I saw something familiar: a tall narrow arch with three high keystones showing boldly against the sky in a fanlike curve. In Central Park terms: the Glen Span.

Our river disappeared into a small, deep pool at its foot, except for a tidy stream that ran on back inside the tunnel under the Span. Through the arch, facing us, lay Central Park and home—just a blur of sunlit green from here.

I was caught between two opposite waves of homesickness as we rode around the pool: for the beauty and grandeur of the Fayre Farre, and for the modest wildness of Central Park. It felt as if my heart was being squeezed in a bone cage.

Our escort began milling around us at the foot of the arch, restless with expectant energy.

Claudia sighed and clambered down off her seelim, giving her mount a regretful pat on its purple shoulder. Rachel and I dismounted too. My blue-green seelim put its head down and rubbed its closed eye on my hip, almost knocking me over. Was this affection, or did it think I was a tree?

Kevin, still mounted, said in a public-address voice, "The princesses want to leave us, friends, through this mystery gate. But do we want them to leave?"

Whoa, my heart bumped hard.

No one answered Kevin's question. Seelims licked the air with their long black tongues for clues to the cause of the tension.

"Didn't we sing them onto the jeweled thrones from the hoard of Dravud Bloodhand last night?" Kevin went on, with a devilish gleam in his eyes. "Didn't we take them to ourselves with all the joy of our victorious hearts?"

"Kevin," I said, low and angry, "don't spoil things, okay?"

"Who's spoiling anything?" Kevin said, looking down at me with a smile. "Not me. But I don't think it's very nice of you and your friends, rejecting our hospitality."

Claudia was already halfway through the archway and there was nothing languid and gliding about her gait, either. She was trotting.

Rachel, right behind her and running backward, waved at me. "Amy, come on! What are you waiting for?"

Before I could make a move, Kevin jumped off his seelim and dashed into the arch ahead of me. He turned and stood there, barring my way.

"Why go anywhere?" he said. "You're a princess here and a brave warrior. The elves make up songs about you."

I stood there, paralyzed between panic and a sneaky surge of pure delight.

Kevin the Corner Kid, the bane of my childhood, was offering me a high destiny. Heck, Rachel and Claudia could be best friends instead of Rachel and me. My mom and dad would never get to skin me alive for vanishing overnight. And I would never have to look at Uncle Irv and Aunt Jennie and my icky little cousins again, or go live in blonde, skinny Los Angeles.

Two elves sang their strange music, with words I somehow understood: "Stay, lend us your powers. We know who the true Champion is: she who slew Famisher Kram."

Danu called out good humoredly, "Stay awhile, you can always go home later, Lady."

Lady? Princess? Slayer of Kram? I had a rich identity here. At home, I was a ninth grader.

"Amy!" Claudia screamed. "He's doing a spell on you, don't you feel it?"

Was he? I stepped forward and felt something like tiny threads breaking all around me in the air.

Kevin said, "What about your Cousin Shelly?"

I was speechless. Somehow, this was the subject I dreaded the most, the subject I had carefully not been thinking about since the battle.

"You meant to remind me," he said. "Don't pretend you don't want to. I said I'd bring her back if you helped, and I will, as soon as my powers are all gathered back to me. It's already started to happen. Very soon, I'll make you a present of her life as the promised reward to a brave and faithful princess."

A rush of hope and longing swept through me, and my eyes filled up with tears.

"I will do it," he said softly. "I will do it for you at moon-rise this very night."

And I knew that he would, and that he could. He had made this whole place, after all.

But Cousin Shelly wasn't part of it. She wasn't a fictional character in Kevin's saga. She had been a real person.

"You never knew her, Kevin," I began.

"You'll show her to me," he answered quickly. "She'll be as real as your memories of her, and how much realer can you get?"

I blinked and looked away from him. Scarneck was watching me curiously.

My memories? But look at my memories of Kevin himself. Look how cockeyed and incomplete they had been—still were, even with all the new things I had learned. Other people knew Shelly differently than I did. I'd heard my relatives talking enough to know, if I cared to admit it, that she wasn't only what I recalled. She'd had a life of her own, out of my sight or beyond my notice or understanding. And that life was over.

I stood wavering between dread and yearning. What would Shelly be like in the kingdom of Kevin Malone? Did I want a phantom Shelly living here in the Fayre Farre, a cartoon all sweet and funny, as Kevin's father had been all cruel and hateful?

The rhinestone pin she'd given me, that had saved our lives just yesterday—that had been the real force of Shelly acting in Kevin's world. Her love had been here, her roses still were.

Sadly, I felt my heart open and I let her go.

I could hardly stand to look at poor Kevin. It seemed to me now that the victorious young prince he had made of himself here had only been trying to get *something* good at long last from his horrible father.

Maybe he would have to keep on trying over and over in different ways forever, because beating the White One wasn't really what he'd wanted at all. What he really wanted would never be there in his memory of the man, because it had never been given.

I blinked my eyes to clear them and tried to answer in a neutral tone. "No, Kevin. I'm sure you can do it and I thank you for the offer, but I've thought it over, and I don't want you to bring my cousin Shelly back."

He seemed to rear up, his eyes gleaming fiercely at me from the gloom of the tunnel. "You don't know what you want! Well, I do. You want to stay here in the Fayre Farre and be a princess and have your cousin alive again. Only you can't accept all that from a kid from the poor end of your old block!"

Then Scarneck stooped and let loose a moorim from— not an ordinary leather bag, but Claudia's PursePet, which was slung from his coppery shoulder. Claudia must have given it to him before she took off through the Glen Span. The moorim darted into the archway and ran up Kevin's clothes without Kevin even noticing. Small red eyes peered at me from Kevin's dark hair.

And whatever Kevin meant to say, what he said to me now was this, and it was the truth: "How do I know I'm real or anything is real without somebody real here with me? I'm afraid. Stay, Amy, help me remember my real life so it doesn't melt away. Help me remember it better. You have to stay. *I'll make you stay*—"

Flushed with fury, he clamped his lips shut and grabbed for the moorim. But the little animal leaped down and scurried back to the Brangleman, who scooped it up from the ground and disappeared into the watching crowd.

Kevin set his feet wide apart. "I don't have to let you go if I don't want to."

"That's plain treachery, Kevin! Get out of my way."

"Make me," he jeered.

God, didn't anything ever really change? It was just like old times: Rotten Kevin standing between me and what I wanted, Kevin who was strong and mean, Kevin the bully, the Corner Kid. I looked anxiously around for help.

"I'm King of the whole Fayre Farre," Kevin declared, "by right of arms and by force of prophecy, and what I say goes. Everyone will do what I tell them."

The audience of battered warriors and amused-looking elves watched closely but kept out of it. Who could blame them? They were the ones who were going to have to live with Prince Kavian. Probably most of them thought I ought to stay. Only Scarneck had dared take a risk for me.

And why had he, that dry, skeptical Brangleman, done that?

Because I was worth it. I'd brought the Farsword, killed Kram, helped Kevin defeat his horrible enemy. Things did change. I wasn't Kevin's little victim anymore, a victim he could terrorize and tyrannize over. Those days were over.

Scarcely breathing, I uprooted my feet again and made them march me toward the tunnel.

Kevin didn't budge. But something enormous moved in the shadows inside the Span, close beside him.

"WHAT'S THAT?" I said, stopping dead.

Kevin laughed scornfully. "I'm supposed to turn and look so you can zip by me? You used to run pretty fast, for a girl. Well, no way. I won't fall for—"

A huge, squat figure, ugly as a gargoyle off a French cathedral, stepped quietly from an opening in the stream-side wall of the arch and picked Kevin up, pinning his arms to his sides and lifting him straight up off the ground.

Kevin said, "Yagghh!" He kicked his feet wildly a yard above the water.

The army behind me gasped and gabbled, but they hung back.

The creature's scaly skin gleamed, and it gave off a dank, fishy smell. Or maybe that was its breath; it had opened its mouth. Kevin's head was going to get bitten off in front of everybody!

From the other end of the arch Claudia called, "Amy, it's all right! It's one of the ones that towed our boat to North Isle for the battle!"

Tenderly, the monster lipped Kevin's hair and then turned its huge face and rubbed its cheek caressingly on the top of Kevin's head.

Kevin kicked harder, shouting, "Smelly, stupid troll, put me down!"

I walked up to the troll breathing shallow breaths. The creature ignored me completely. I looked up at suspended Kevin. He glared back down at me murderously.

I said, "Kevin, listen. I did my stuff here; I did what you asked me to. I don't want rewards, I want to go home. And I'm going."

He quit struggling and concentrated on swearing furiously at me. I could just make out a ragged-edged cave in the side wall where several smaller trolls clustered, peeking out with glowing eyes.

When Kevin paused for breath I said, "I'm going, and I want a decent good-bye."

"Go ahead, then!" he yelled, raising hollow echoes in the archway. "Run home like a baby, I don't care!"

"You think that's good enough?" I asked. I believe I actually stamped my foot. "I don't. That sounds to me like Anglower's nasty, spiteful son, not like a Promised Champion, a hero of battle, a ruling prince of the Fayre Farre!"

Silence. I folded my arms, which were covered with goose bumps. I sneezed. It was cold, damp, and odorous in there with Kevin and his troll, and I couldn't wait to get done with all of it. But I waited.

Kevin growled, "All right. Thanks for your help, and good luck to you." Then he added craftily, "But you have to pay for your passage. It's customary to give these bridge trolls something—or else they take an arm, or a leg. Mine, this time. On your account."

I didn't believe he was in any danger from the adoring troll that held him, but how could I know for certain? And I did have money, coin of the realm. Singer's silver gift burned cold in my hand.

Kevin must have read something in my eyes.

"Amy, don't go," he said. He relaxed against the troll's warty shoulder. "Look how ugly she is." His voice was rough with wry affection. "I made her that way. However they are, I made them all. I can't walk out on them. You can—but you don't have to. You could stay. You could see what wonderful things I'll do here to make up for all this pain and trouble."

"You'll do great," I said, hoping with all my heart that it was true. "I don't have to see it to know it, Kevin."

I pitched the coin into the water right under Kevin's feet. The troll, her gaze caught by the bright movement, forgot she was holding him and let go. He landed with a squawk on all fours, in water up to his forearms.

That's how I remember the Promised Champion most clearly: picking himself up with water streaming from his sleeves, his expression unreadable in the dimness under the arch. The troll was hunkered down beside him paddling around in the water, looking for the shiny thing that had fallen there.

I jogged on to the west end of the Glen Span, where Rachel and Claudia waited in the sunlight of an April day in New York City.

>—◆—<

Never again, I told my parents: it was all done and would never happen again. Rachel and Claudia and I had wandered around the city together overnight by way of helping me say good-bye to my Manhattan childhood. That was the story we told. My parents believed it. And, in a way, it was true.

Mom put me in charge of all of Shelly's plants, which is supposed to be a chore but I like it. Taped to one of the pots I found a postcard somebody sent Shelly of a cactus, one of those round ones covered with fine hair like a moorim's fur, in the Huntington Gardens. Mom says that's a world-famous botanical garden that Shelly always wanted to visit. It's in Los Angeles, and Shelly never got there. But I will.

I'd say I got off lightly. Claudia was instantly grounded for life, more or less. She acts as if nothing happened, which I guess is one way to handle it. Mostly she is into some heavy studying in science. She says she's thinking seriously of trying to get into veterinary school.

She brought something home with her, something from the Fayre Farre: a rose she picked on the mountaintop. It's in a jelly jar of water on her windowsill, as fresh as that day she picked it, which strikes me as creepy.

"Maybe she should have left it," I told Rachel.

We were lying on my bed reading a copy of ArtScene, *a weekly paper that Dad had brought back from Los Angeles. Rachel's parents had docked her entire allowance. She can't go shopping, so she's been spending more time at my house. She has also taken up karate. Of all the people to go in for martial arts! She says she loves it.*

She tapped her pen against her teeth and kept skimming the personals. Rachel loves to read the personals, any personals. "Claudia says not to worry about it," she said. "The rose isn't really a flower, it's like, a symbol. Don't you get it? The roses were time. Solving 'the riddle of using the years' meant figuring out that your brooch was the key to the roses, and the roses were stored-up years. They smothered Anglower in all the time it would have taken for real roses to grow and cover that whole mountain right down to the plains. Time was the only cure for all the bad memories of his miserable father that Kevin carried around. Maybe Claudia needs time like that, too. So she took the flower."

She circled an ad in red ink. " 'Prepare to meet the woman of your dreams.' Do they really talk like that out there?"

"Guess I'll find out," I said. I knew the plans were all made. We were moving first thing this summer, when school was over.

"Hey, we could send code messages through the personals," Rachel said. She nudged me. "Look, I'm sorry if I've been, you know, bitchy to you. Your parents are the ones who decided to leave, not you. It just felt like—well, it's hard losing your best friend. It makes you act pissy. But you can't blame me for hanging out with other people because you're going to be gone."

"At least you knew Claudia from before, a little," I said, feeling sorry for myself. "I've got to make all new friends somehow, in a place almost as weird as the Fayre Farre. At least in Kevin's country people do sometimes WALK from point A to point B."

Later I thought, hadn't Scarneck and Singer become my friends? Didn't the moorim give up its life for us three girls, me included? If I could make friends in Kevin Malone's kingdom, I could make friends anywhere.

I had even made a friend, sort of, out of Kevin. I think about him sometimes.

What I think about most is that as long as the rose that Claudia picked just sits in its jar without changing, it means that the White One is still safely buried under Shelly's roses, on top of a mountain in Kevin's Fayre Farre.